Danny And The Dinosaurs

By Lizak Strahm

Illustrated by Magdalena Su

This is a work of fiction. Names, characters, places and incidents either are the product of the author's imagination or are used fictitiously, and any resemblance to any persons, living or dead, business establishments, events or locales is entirely coincidental.

DANNY AND THE DINOSAURS

Published by Sinic Publishing.
Copyright © 2013 by Simon Forsyth (writing as Lizak Strahm).
Cover art by Jaw Adams.

ISBN: 1484839641
ISBN-13: 9781484839645

LizakStrahm.com

First Printing: January, 2014.
Printed in the United States of America by Createspace.

First edition: January, 2014.

For Alan

Contents

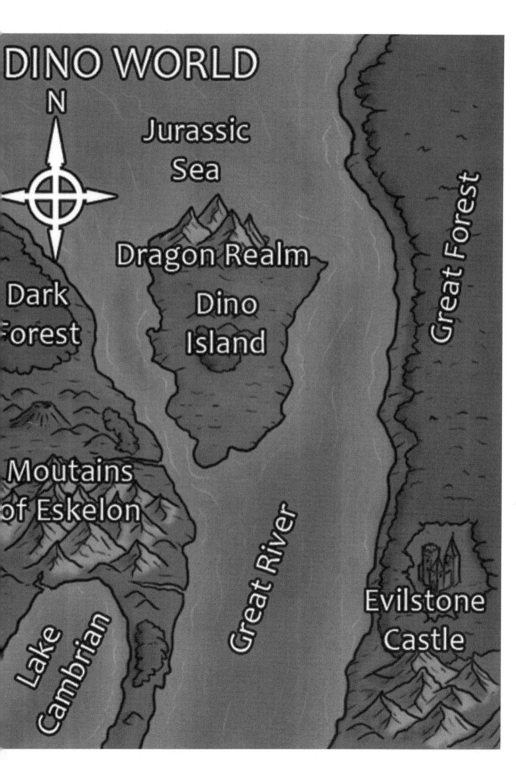

A Surprise
For Danny

The enormous T. rex lifted its gigantic head and roared at the soldier who was stood trembling on the ground before him.

'*Raaaar!*' it bellowed. Its razor sharp talons lifted high into the air - ready to strike down upon its defenseless prey.

It was very, very hungry. And it was now dinner time!

The soldier, with nothing but a battered old sword to protect himself and a rusty old helmet stuck fast to his head, gave out a yell of terror.

'*Arrrgh!*' he cried as he saw the T. rex 's enormous mouth opening wide, it's jagged teeth glinting menacingly in the sun.

The soldier hastily looked around for an escape route, his eyes darting left and right as he quickly scanned his surroundings.

Danny And The Dinosaurs

Over there, by the tree! Hope suddenly filled his heart as he spotted the welcoming shelter of some rocks a short distance away. But could he make it in time? There was only one way to find out!

He sprang forwards and began sprinting as fast as he could towards his stony refuge, his legs and arms a whirl of panic-stricken movement.

'Raaaar!' the dinosaur bellowed as it made a mighty leap towards him and quickly gave chase, jaws snapping and feet pounding furiously through the long grass...

THUMP! SNAP! THUMP! SNAP! THUMP! SNAP!

Closer and closer it got, the ground trembling beneath its huge and powerful feet.

'Nearly there now, just keep going!' gasped the soldier to himself as he strained every muscle and sinew in his body to reach the sanctuary of the rocks before it was too late.

THUMP! SNAP! THUMP! SNAP! THUMP! SNAP!

The soldier continued on, racing over the thick grass for all he was worth; leaping over fallen branches and scrambling around giant bushes and shrubs.

Then he suddenly began to feel the dinosaur's hot breath on the back of his head!

'Faster, faster!' the soldier urged himself, summoning all his remaining strength to push his body onwards and away from the rapidly advancing threat.

He quickly changed direction and darted off to his left, then his right, then his left again in a frantic effort to throw the dinosaur off his tail.

A Surprise For Danny

'*Raaaar!*' came the booming bellow behind him, so close now that the soldier thought his ear-drums would burst.

Then, with one last effort, the soldier dived for the rocks, almost breathless with fear. The dinosaur, just meters behind, suddenly threw itself into the air behind him and made a last desperate snap with its jaws at its fleeing prey.

SNAP!

It missed!

Just in time, the soldier scrambled to safety.

Phew!

Danny put his toy dinosaur and soldier down on the lawn.

Maybe next time he'd have the soldier fighting the dinosaur with his sword and chopping its head off. Yes - that would be cool!

He gazed at the plastic dinosaur lying in the grass. *If only it were real,* he thought. *If only it wasn't just a toy.*

He sighed and leaned back into the soft grass, staring up at the blue skies and the hot sun burning overhead.

What he wouldn't give to see a *real, live* dinosaur, like the ones his Uncle Felix was always showing him in the pictures of his textbooks.

His Uncle Felix was what was called a palaeontologist. That's a scientist who travels all over the world finding dinosaur fossils and digging them up out of the ground.

His uncle had been away in Africa on one of his many fossil hunting expeditions and Danny hadn't seen him for many months. Danny was looking forward to seeing him again - especially since his uncle would have many exciting dinosaur bones to show him when he got back!

It amazed Danny that fossils still existed after being buried for millions upon millions of years beneath dirt, dust and rocks. *Dinosaur bones must be very well made,* he thought. *And to think, dinosaurs last roamed the earth before human beings even existed!*

He gazed high up into the sky and watched as an eagle soared majestically between the clouds. *Just think,* Danny thought to himself, *millions and millions of years ago that wouldn't be an eagle flying up there. It would be a flying dinosaur! Probably a pterodactyl or a peteinosaurus.*

Danny knew a lot of dinosaur names. He had lots of books about them and had learned the names off by heart. Some names were really hard to read though, so he copied the words into a little notebook and whenever he visited his uncle he showed them to him and his uncle would tell him how to say the word.

Danny continued to gaze at the eagle, imagining it was a pterodactyl with its massive wings spread out wide by its sides. *Some pterodactyls were as big as a small airplane and had wingspans of over 40 feet.*

Imagine that. That's as long as a bus!

'Danny? Where are you? Your breakfast's ready!'

His mom's shout brought Danny out of his daydream and he jumped to his feet.

'Oh, there you are,' said his mom, coming into the garden. 'What have you been doing out here all this time?'

A Surprise For Danny

Danny leaned down and picked up his toys. 'I've been playing Soldiers and Dinosaurs,' he replied. 'The soldier only just escaped in the nick of time. He found some rocks to hide in just before the dinosaur pounced on him and gobbled him up for its breakfast!'

His mom smiled. 'Well, why don't you come in for *your* breakfast? It's on the table waiting for you. Your dad and I have already finished ours. And you may also be interested to know that we have a surprise for you.'

A surprise? Danny's eyes lit up at the thought. *Perhaps his summer holidays wouldn't be so boring after all.*

Inside, the smell of bacon and eggs hung in the air, making Danny's mouth water. All the playing in the garden had made him starving! While he tucked into a full plate, his mom and dad exchanged amused glances.

'So,' said Danny through mouthfuls of bacon, 'what was it you wanted to tell me?'

His dad winked and said, 'Well, we were thinking of going to your Uncle Felix's today and wondered if you wanted to come?'

Danny shot up out of his seat, almost toppling his orange juice over at the same time. 'Really?!' he exclaimed, an excited grin spreading across his face. 'Uncle Felix is back? When did he get home?'

His mom laughed and started to clear away the dishes. 'Last night. He phoned while you were in bed. And he invited us to stay over for a few days.' She ruffled Danny's hair as she walked past. 'I take it that means you think we should go?'

Danny punched his fist in the air. 'Woo hoo!' he shouted, 'of course it does!'

He gobbled up the rest of his breakfast as fast as he could and then ran upstairs to get his things ready.

Danny flew around his bed room, gathering all the tools he would need for his stay with his Uncle Felix. His uncle often showed him his fossils and sometimes he even let Danny clean them. So he made sure he packed his special brush for taking dust and dirt off the fossils and searched all of his cupboards until he found his magnifying glass, which would allow him to look really closely at each item. Then, just to be sure, he packed a cloth, a notepad and some pencils. There was surely going to be a lot to learn during his stay!

'Danny are you ready?' called his mom from downstairs.

'Coming!' he shouted back, grabbing his bag and running downstairs.

'Got everything you need?' asked his dad.

'Sure do,' said Danny.

'There's one other thing I forgot to tell you,' said his mom as they all headed outside.

'What is it?' asked Danny.

Mom smiled as she locked the front door and led him towards the car, where his dad was starting up the engine. 'Well,' she said, 'don't tell your father I told you, but your Uncle Felix has a present for you.' She smiled and held a finger up to her lips. 'But, sshhh, it's our secret!'

A Surprise For Danny

A secret?! Thought Danny as he climbed into the back seat of the car. *Wow! I wonder what it could be?*

The journey to his Uncle Felix's house was a long one and Danny could barely sit still in his seat he was so excited. He couldn't believe his uncle had brought him back a present. He only got presents on his birthday or at Christmas, so this present must be something extra special indeed.

A long time later, the car finally slowed and they turned into a long, gravel driveway. Danny peered out of the window at the huge house in the distance, his nose pressed up to the glass. Uncle Felix's house was one of his favorite places in the whole world. It had a mysterious, almost magical feel to it when you were inside.

The old house was like a rabbit warren, full of winding corridors and interesting rooms that contained many weird and wonderful objects that his uncle had collected during his adventures around the world. Wood lined passageways criss-crossed the whole house and there was even a secret room hidden behind a false wall.

It had the biggest windows and doors Danny had ever seen in a house and a tall roof that was so high a family of pigeons nested in it.

Danny's eyes lingered on the top windows of the attic, where his uncle kept a lot of his dinosaur finds safely stored in glass cabinets and boxes. A shiver ran over his skin and as soon as the car stopped, he jumped outside.

Danny And The Dinosaurs

'Don't forget your bag!' said his dad.

Danny trotted back, grabbed it, and then began running excitedly towards the front stairs that led to the large oak front door of his uncle's house.

A Surprise For Danny

'Uncle Felix, Uncle Felix - we're here!' he shouted excitedly as he darted up the steep steps. Just as he reached the top, the door slowly pulled inwards and his uncle appeared in the opening.

Danny And The Dinosaurs

He was a very tall man, even taller than Danny's dad. And largely built, like a big grizzly bear. A wide brimmed hat was perched on top of his head, and he was wearing a brown safari style shirt which gave him the appearance of Indiana Jones from the famous Hollywood movies.

Danny dropped his bag and opened his arms as he rushed towards his uncle.

'Well, well, well!' said Uncle Felix as he gave Danny a great big hug. 'You're just in time.'

'In time for what?' asked Danny.

His uncle grinned at him and ushered him inside. 'Why your surprise, that's what!'

An Unexpected Present

While Mom and Dad were busy unpacking the suitcases, Uncle Felix took Danny up the long winding staircase that led to the large attic at the very top of the house.

Uncle Felix led the way, with Danny close behind, their footsteps making loud clumping sounds on the bare wooden boards as they climbed.

Thin bands of light filtered in from the windows. A mouse scuttled across the wooden floor, making Danny jump.

'Oh don't worry about Bobby,' said Uncle Felix. 'He usually hides in the walls.'

'Bobby?' asked Danny.

His uncle smiled. 'That's the mouse's name.'

A bubble of laughter escaped Danny's lips. *Uncle Felix sure was a funny old thing!*

Danny And The Dinosaurs

As they approached the top of the staircase, Uncle Felix stopped and looked at Danny. His big blue eyes were grave and serious now, and he had a small frown.

'Now listen, Danny,' he said. 'This present of yours is very precious and valuable, so you must promise me something first.'

'What is it?' Danny asked.

'You must promise to never treat the present I am going to give you as a toy. It's a very important item. You must be very, very careful with it.'

Danny bobbed his head. 'I promise,' he said, trying hard not to burst with excitement.

Uncle Felix wagged his finger at him. 'I'm serious, Danny. This is not a toy.' He then pulled a large, brass key from his pocket. 'But I know I can trust you,' he added with a warm smile.

As Uncle Felix unlocked the door, Danny's heart thudded hard in his chest. Uncle Felix's' faith in him to look after something so precious was a great honor, and the fact that his uncle trusted him so much made Danny glow with pride.

The door creaked open and he followed his uncle inside, their footsteps making the old wooden floorboards moan with each step.

The room they entered was enormous, with a large picture window in the far wall that gave a bird's eye view of the rolling countryside beyond. Tall bookcases lined the walls on either side, stuffed with dusty old textbooks and manuscripts.

An Unexpected Present

On the far side of the room were several glass cabinets which were filled with different types of fossils and scraps of bones in glass boxes.

And all around on the floor of this huge room were piled various boxes, all labeled with long names that Danny couldn't pronounce. These were filled with some of the fossils his uncle had just brought back from Africa to study.

Danny stopped at a large rectangular table which stood at the other end of the room. On top of it was a large, oval-shaped object covered in a black cloth.

'What's under the cloth, Uncle Felix?' asked Danny.

Uncle Felix tapped his nose. 'Promise you will take care of it?'

'What, you mean this is my present?!'

A broad grin crept across Uncle Felix's face and his deep blue eyes began to twinkle. 'Yes!'

'Oh, gosh!' said Danny, his heart pounding in his chest. 'Yes, I promise I'll take care of it.'

His uncle's grin grew wider, and his eyes gave an extra little twinkle.

'What is it, Uncle Felix? pleaded Danny. 'Oh, please tell me!'

His uncle chuckled, enjoying Danny's suspense and excitement.

'Okay then,' he said after a pause so long Danny thought his heart would explode.

And with those words, he whipped back the black cloth.

And there it was!

Danny's eyes widened in surprise. There, on the table in front of him, was an egg the size of a football. Although it was covered in a lot of dirt, he could see that it was a deep green color. In fact, it was the deepest green he had ever seen.

An Unexpected Present

'Is that a...'

'Yes, it's a dinosaur egg! Well the fossil of an egg,' said Uncle Felix.

'Can I touch it?'

'Not at the moment. I haven't had time to clean it yet,' replied Uncle Felix as he placed a pair of gold-rimmed glasses on his nose. He then bent down and peered at it closely. 'So, Danny, what do you think?'

'It's amazing! What sort of dinosaur egg is it?'

'Well, that's the very curious thing about this egg,' his uncle replied, a perplexed expression crossing over his face. 'I have no idea.'

'You don't?'

'No. I have never come across a dinosaur egg like this one before. For a start, it's rounder than any other dinosaur egg I have ever come across. Secondly, it's bigger than any other dinosaur egg that has ever been found before - we checked the records. The previous biggest egg was around 19 inches tall - this one is 41 inches!'

'Wow! That's a big difference.'

'Yes, it certainly is. And the other curious thing about it - and the *most* curious thing - is its color.'

'Why?'

'Well, no one has ever found a *green* dinosaur egg before.'

'Haven't they?'

'No. Just look at it.'

Danny leaned forward and stared again at the egg. His eyes fell upon its smooth curves and then followed the tiny lines and contours that marked the stony surface. It was laced with tiny holes, crevices and grooves that had been etched into it during the millions of years it had lain undisturbed in the rocks of the great African rainforest.

But the most striking thing about it, as Danny had observed when his eyes had first set sight upon it, was the color. It captivated him. A deep, luxuriant green that almost seemed to shimmer slightly in the light from the window.

And then, as he stared harder at it, he thought he could see the green actually moving across the surface of the egg! It didn't move for very long, just for a split second. But it was long enough for Danny's keen eyes to notice.

He blinked, thinking his eyes were slightly out of focus from staring too long. He looked again.

Nothing.

The color was as still and motionless as a statue.

Hmmm, it must have been just a trick of the light, thought Danny.

He continued to gaze at the egg, marveling at its size and shape - closely examining the long crevices and deep grooves. He was spell bound.

This was without a doubt the best present he had ever had - and that included the PlayStation he had received for his last birthday!

Uncle Felix looked at Danny's mesmerized expression and smiled broadly. 'I'll leave you to it,' he said as he stood up. He patted Danny gently on the head, walked over to one of the book shelves and began searching for a book he wanted.

But Danny had barely heard his Uncle's words. He was too bewitched by the egg. He continued to stare at it intently, his eyeballs glued to the ancient fossil.

Oh, how he wished that he could touch it. To take it in his hands and feel the surface with his fingers. But he knew that he had to be patient and wait for his uncle to clean it.

Then, a sudden gasp escaped from his lips as a portion of green color suddenly moved slightly over the surface of the bottom corner of the egg. Again, the movement only lasted for a moment, but Danny was sure of it this time. He rubbed his eyes and looked again.

It *was* moving!

The green color swirled and rippled, becoming darker in the thin lines and grooves and then twinkling brightly as it crept out again on to the smoother part of the egg's surface.

Then the whole egg shook slightly and twitched!

Danny jumped back in his seat with shock.

'Uncle!' he cried, moving his head back in surprise. 'Look at the egg, it's… it's moving!'

Uncle Felix, who was busily leafing through the text book he'd found, looked over towards Danny.

'Huh?'

'The egg just moved! And the green color is swirling about on its surface!'

Uncle Felix put the book down on the shelf and walked back towards Danny. He stopped at the table and then bent down to peer carefully through his glasses at the egg.

'Hmmm… It looks perfectly still to me. And I can't see the color moving or anything.'

'What?!'

Danny quickly looked back down at the egg again.

His uncle was right! The egg just lay there on the table, as still as could be. And the deep green color was now as motionless as dry paint.

Uncle Felix gave Danny a quizzical look.

'But the egg *did* move Uncle - honest!' protested Danny. 'And the green *was* swishing about. It was like treacle. And when it ran into the little grooves and crevices it went darker and then lighter and then it kind of twinkled.'

Danny knew by the look his uncle was now giving him that he didn't believe a word he was saying.

'Okay, I think you've been staring at that egg long enough now.' His uncle chuckled. 'I think your imagination is starting to run away with you a little.'

'But it *wasn't* my imagination!' pleaded Danny. He stared down at the egg again, willing it with all his might to do something that would prove to his uncle that what he had seen was real.

The egg, however, seemed to have other ideas. It just continued to sit there, stock-still, like a statue.

'C'mon Danny, we better cover it up now and go back downstairs to see your parents. It's almost dinner time and I'm sure they'll be very hungry.'

An Unexpected Present

'Oh, alright then,' mumbled Danny, still peeved that Uncle Felix didn't believe him.

He carefully placed the black cloth back over the egg and walked over to the door where his uncle was waiting for him.

As he made his way back downstairs again, Danny was deep in thought about the mysterious egg and what it had done.

He hadn't imagined it. He was sure of that! There was no doubt about it - there was something very, very strange about that egg.

Something almost... magical...

The Strangest Thing Happens

Dinner flew by. So caught up in thinking about the egg, Danny hardly even tasted his soup or the roast beef his uncle had cooked. Even when the apple pie was brought out, Danny barely stirred from scratching away in his notepad, drawing out quick but accurate pictures of the mysterious green egg.

'What are you doing?' asked his mom as she took a second helping of pie.

Danny just shrugged and mumbled 'nothing,' his pen sketching over the pad quicker and quicker.

That night, curled up in bed, Danny couldn't sleep. The thought of the egg and its strange and mysterious behavior had him tossing and turning more times than a washing machine.

What had caused the green color to move and swirl across its surface? Why had it done it? And what had caused the egg to suddenly jump and twitch?

Danny And The Dinosaurs

The questions kept buzzing around and around in his head and just wouldn't go away.

Eventually, unable to get even a moment's rest, Danny pulled back his covers and got out of bed. The chill in the air wrapped around him like an icy blanket. *Darn! He should have brought his dressing gown with him from home.*

He thought about what to do and decided perhaps it would be best to get changed into the clothes he had been wearing that day as they were warmer than his flimsy pajamas.

As soon as he was dressed, he made towards the bedroom door. He just *had* to go and see the egg. Then a thought struck him. He looked around the dark room, lit only by the light from the moon streaming in through the window.

Perhaps he should give the egg a clean? That should make it easier to see when the color moved again. And after all, it did look pretty grubby. Uncle Felix had mentioned he hadn't had the time to do it himself yet.

Grabbing the brush and cloth he'd packed in his bag, Danny headed out of the room.

The hallway was pitch dark and he had to feel his way along the wall so that he didn't walk into anything. His parents and Uncle Felix were downstairs watching the television, but he didn't turn on the light in case one of them happened to walk past the stairs and notice it was on.

They would only want to know why he wasn't fast asleep in bed. Adults had the most annoying habit of always asking awkward questions you didn't particularly want to give them the answer to!

The Strangest Thing Happens

He crept along very quietly, his arms stretched out straight in front of him, like a mummy in one of those old Hollywood horror films. As he passed the bathroom another thought hit him. He'd need some sort of liquid or cream to clean the egg with. But what to use?

He quietly crept into the bathroom. The door to the bathroom cabinet creaked complainingly on its hinges as he pulled it open and then a small light popped on. Inside were various bottles and jars. Danny peered at one of the labels.

Warto-Zap Wart Remover, it said. *Hmm, that's no good.* He looked at another one. Smelly-Nice Aftershave For Men. *No good either! What about this one?* He twisted a big brown bottle around so he could read what it said. Gleamy-Bright Mouthwash Solution. *Definitely not!*

Danny rummaged through the rest of the bottles and was losing any hope of finding something suitable to clean the egg with until his hand came upon a small, blue jar. Danny picked it up and read the label.

This is what it said:

Time Travel Anti-Aging Face Cream

For a younger you! This amazing skin cream cleans and nourishes the skin and is the night time answer to a healthy, youthful looking face.

Danny And The Dinosaurs

Simply apply the cream before you go to bed and in the morning you will be astonished at how much younger you will look. It's as if you've traveled back in time!

Surely this will make the egg look better, thought Danny.

He could barely contain his glee as he tucked the jar into his trouser pocket and carefully made his way up the steps leading to the attic.

At the top, he had to stand on his tiptoes to reach the brass key Uncle Felix had placed on the shelf. He grasped it in his hand and then placed it in the lock and clicked it open. He then turned the door handle and quietly pushed the big wooden door open.

The attic felt even colder than the rest of the house and Danny felt a shiver run up his spine as he quietly closed the door behind him.

All was still and silent, except for the slight sound of the wind as it whistled past the big window at the far side of the room. The full moon was visible outside, bright and clear like a dazzling searchlight. It flooded parts of the room in rippling pools of shimmery light.

Danny's eyes fell upon the table, grey and dark in the shadows at the other side of the room. He smiled and tiptoed over, the floorboards creaking in protest with every step.

He put down the brush and cloth he'd brought with him and then removed the black cover from the egg.

The Strangest Thing Happens

He stared in wonder at the green object, sitting there quite still upon the table top. *Wow!* he thought, *a real dinosaur egg. Just think, millions upon millions of years ago some great big mommy dinosaur laid that. And now, after lying around for all that time, it was here - sitting right upon the table top in his Uncle Felix's attic. And what's more, it was now his egg!*

Danny wondered about the kind of dinosaur that had laid it. *Had it been a great big ferocious dinosaur with teeth the size of elephant tusks and big, sharp claws like 'Wolverine' from 'X-Men'? Was it a dangerous meat-eater that chased through the forests after other dinosaurs and ate them all up in one big bite ? Or was it a plant eating dinosaur that just wandered around the great plains of Africa eating the grass and plants?*

Danny hoped that his uncle would one day be able to identify the type of dinosaur egg it was. *It sure would be cool to find out.*

With great care, he picked the egg up from the table and then sat down on the floor. Crossing his legs, he gently cradled the large fossil in his lap. Wow, it certainly was heavy!

Danny then took out his brush and set about very carefully brushing off the dust and dirt that coated the outer layer of the egg.

It took almost ten minutes to get most of the dust and dirt off, but when he'd finished, the deep vibrant green was even more dazzling than before. As Danny moved the egg around in his hands, the moonlight danced upon the surface, glimmering and glinting a thousand shades of green as he did so.

Danny And The Dinosaurs

The egg seemed to be alive with sparkling color. Danny gazed down in wonder at this ancient fossil that seemed to be as old as time itself.

Picking up his cloth from the floor, Danny opened the jar of *Time Travel Night Cream* and dabbed the cloth inside. This should make it look even better! he thought.

With slow, deliberate circles he started to polish the egg. It took some time for the cream to penetrate the hard surface, but after a while Danny could start to see a new layer of the egg emerging underneath as even more of the dirt came off.

He continued on, but it was a slow process. He would have to spend quite a few minutes dabbing, circling and wiping before he had worked through the last stubborn layer of grime and dirt. And that was just a tiny area about the size of a nickel.

On and on he worked for what seemed like hours, until - finally - he had cleaned the entire surface of the egg until it gleamed like a precious jewel.

'Perfect,' he whispered to himself as he set it down upon the floor.

And then the strangest and most surprising thing began to happen...

Falling Into
The Past

Danny gasped and watched in astonishment as the egg suddenly began to shudder and shake!

Rat-a-tat-tat! it went as it shook violently against the wooden floorboards. Danny scrambled backwards in shock, his eyes glued to the egg.

It then suddenly rolled to one side, the moonlight glancing off the green shell in glistening bursts. Danny couldn't stop staring. And then, right before his very eyes, the egg began to grow!

Bigger and bigger it stretched…

… The size of a beach ball…

… The size of a dog kennel…

Bit by bit the egg warped and distorted, growing ever bigger by the second. Then a tiny crack appeared in the side and a rumbling, crackling sound suddenly echoed through the room as the egg continued to grow and grow and grow…

Danny And The Dinosaurs

As tall as a pony…

As tall as a man…

Shivers ran up and down Danny's arms. He couldn't believe his eyes. He rubbed at them furiously. *Was he still sleeping? Was this a dream? No, it couldn't be; it felt too real.*

The egg kept on growing and growing and growing. Danny continued to watch in amazement as the crack in the shell opened up to form a large hole. A hole big enough for a small boy to fit through.

And then finally, with one last, gigantic shudder, the egg's amazing growth spurt came to an abrupt stop. Silence filled the air once more, the egg now as motionless and still as a statue.

It was now over six feet tall and wider than a door!

Danny sat there, frozen to the spot. *Had the adults heard the strange sounds emanating from the egg as it grew?* He waited, listening for any footsteps clattering on the stairs outside as they came scurrying up to see what all the commotion had been about.

The attic was a long way up from the living room where his parents and Uncle Felix were watching television, so it was doubtful they had heard anything. But Danny still waited. One minute passed… Two… When he was sure no one coming, he got to his feet.

His hand shook as he nervously reached out to touch the smooth shell of the giant egg. It felt hard and warm under his fingertips. Suddenly a thought struck him. *Was there anything inside this mysterious object? Was a baby dinosaur about to rush out and gobble him up?*

Falling Into The Past

Danny knew this thought sounded silly. *After all, the egg was a fossil and millions of years old. But then again, it had just suddenly grown to the size of a fully grown man right in front of his eyes! So, anything now seemed possible.*

He took a deep breath, leaned closer and peered into the large hole in the side.

Darkness swirled before his eyes and Danny couldn't see a thing. He put his hand up to his ear and listened... Nothing.

He paused in thought for a moment. *Should he run downstairs and tell his parents and Uncle Felix what had happened? Or should he investigate the inside of the egg first and find out if there was anything inside?*

He then recalled what had happened earlier that day when he had seen the color moving across the egg's surface and when it had twitched and moved about on the table top. Yet, when his Uncle Felix had come over, the egg had acted perfectly normally!

What if he did go downstairs and told the adults what had just happened? What if they all came upstairs to have a look at the egg and it was back to its normal size again? Of course, they would all think he was being naughty and making things up. Not only would he get in trouble for that, but he'd also get told off for being out of bed.

That settled it then!

He'd see if there was anything inside the egg now, and then go back to bed. He'd just let his Uncle Felix find the egg in the morning, and if it was still the size of a man then he couldn't get into trouble for telling tales.

Pulling over a wooden chair from the table, Danny gingerly climbed on top and clasped the sides of the hole with his hands. He wished he had a flashlight with him, but he'd left that at home.

Well, little did he know that he would be exploring the inside of a gigantic dinosaur egg!

Falling Into The Past

Then, with a deep breath, he hoisted himself up and onto the ledge of the hole. Unfortunately, however, he pulled himself up a little too fast and he wobbled precariously at the mouth, almost losing his balance completely and falling in. He tried to correct himself by leaning backwards slightly but his left foot suddenly slipped off the edge, causing him to tilt even further into the dark opening. This jolt of movement then caused his left hand to lose its grip on the edge of the hole and Danny tipped forward beyond the point of no return, plunging head first into the dark, gloomy gap!

'*Arrrgh!*' he yelled as he fell.

Darkness immediately enveloped him like a shadowy blanket.

He tried to brace himself for the inevitable crash onto the hard floor of the egg. But nothing happened. He just continued to fall and fall and fall…

How was this happening? Where was the floor?!

He felt his body spinning around faster and faster as he fell deeper and deeper, further and further down into the black, murky abyss.

As he tumbled, Danny felt a strange tingling sensation taking over his whole body. It spread down his neck to his arms, then his tummy and finally to his legs. It was the most peculiar feeling he had ever experienced. It was like his whole body was fizzing like a can of coke!

On and on and on he fell… Spinning, twisting, rolling, whirling, fizzing…

Was he going to be falling forever?!

Down and down he plunged. Deeper and deeper and deeper...

Spinning, twisting, rolling, whirling, fizzing...

Oh how he wished he'd just gone back to bed!

Down, down, down he continued to plunge...

Spinning, twisting, rolling, whirling, fizzing...

... Or was it down?

Hang on a minute...

... Yes, he was sure - he was now falling to one side. He could feel it. He could definitely feel himself being pulled SIDEWAYS!

Sideways, sideways, sideways, he continued to plunge...

Spinning, twisting, rolling, whirling, fizzing...

Just what on earth was going on?! How can you fall sideways?

Or was it sideways?

Hang on a minute...

Now he felt himself falling UP!

Up?! How can you fall up?!

... But, yes, he was sure - he was definitely falling up. He could feel it. He could definitely feel himself being pulled upwards!

Up, up, up he continued to plunge...

Spinning, twisting, rolling, whirling, fizzing...

Then he felt himself falling down again, then quickly up again!

Up and down, up and down, up and down he continued to plunge...

Spinning, twisting, rolling, whirling, fizzing...

Falling Into The Past

Then suddenly brightness was all around him; a dazzling bright green light that moved and swirled and bubbled in front of his eyes.

Danny felt the tingling sensation in his body begin to ease and he felt his body slowing down. Brightness suddenly filled his eyes and then...

THUMP!

He felt himself land on something soft and squishy and he tumbled forwards, head over heels. He rolled over several times before coming to a stop in a great big heap on the floor.

He lay there motionless for a few seconds, trying to recover from his ordeal. All that spinning and twisting and fizzing had made his head feel quite dizzy.

Eventually he sat up and rubbed his eyes. He then peered at the ground.

It was grass!

'What on earth is going on?' he muttered.

He slowly staggered to his feet and looked around. It was rather dark, but he could make out a big, oval shaped object several meters away. He cautiously walked towards it. *Strange,* he thought. *It seemed to have a hole in the side of it... a hole just big enough for a small boy to fit through...*

... Hang on...

... It can't be...

... IT IS!

Danny stopped in front of the object and stared at it in utter astonishment, his mouth wide open in shock.

It was the dinosaur egg! The very same dinosaur egg that he had just fallen *into* not 5 minutes ago!

How could this be?!

He scratched his head in confusion, trying to make some sense out of this strange and mind-boggling situation.

He had fallen *into* the egg - that he knew. He also knew that he had fallen down, then sideways, then up, then down again and then up and down. And then he had fallen *out* of the egg into this strange place.

But the egg had followed him here - for there it was, as large as life and right in front of his eyes!

Or maybe he had followed the egg?!

He wasn't sure. In fact, he wasn't sure about anything anymore.

Suddenly there was a loud fizzing and crackling noise from the egg. Danny gazed open-mouthed as the hole in the side of the egg began to shrink.

The sides narrowed first with a pinging fizz.

FIZZZZZ!

Then the top and bottom of the hole began to shrink, too. A loud crackling sound filled the air.

CRAAACK!

Danny watched as the hole got smaller and smaller and smaller. Until, finally, the hole disappeared altogether with a whiz-banging pop.

POP!

And it was gone!

The egg, however, remained exactly where it was, sitting perfectly still and as solid as a rock.

Falling Into The Past

Well, whatever next! How was he going to get back to Uncle Felix's now? He couldn't climb back into a hole that wasn't there any more, could he?

He wasn't even sure that climbing back into the hole would have gotten him back to Uncle Felix's anyway.

Things were very confusing!

Danny looked at the egg again and noticed that it was resting against a huge wall. He looked up. And up. And up…

But it wasn't a wall at all… It was the biggest tree trunk he had ever seen. And he was standing right in its shadow, which was so dark it made it hard to tell what it was.

Stepping out into the light, Danny could suddenly see where he was. He gasped in astonishment at the sight which met his eyes.

There, in front of him, lay a dense forest spread out as far as the eye could see. He started to walk forward, gazing around in amazed confusion.

'What *is* this place?' he asked to no one but the huge trees and swaying grass. 'How on earth have I found myself here?!'

But before he had the chance to think of an answer, a huge roar suddenly burst through the air. The giant trees quivered and the leaves shook on their branches. Then, another booming bellow thundered through the forest, a roar so loud and fierce that it made a lion's sound like a small cat in comparison.

Danny ducked behind a nearby tree and peered out into the forest.

'**RAAAR!**' came the great sound. Followed by...

THUMP!

THUMP!

THUMP!

The ground shook violently beneath Danny's feet. So hard in fact, that he nearly fell backwards into a giant shrub behind him. He gasped and gripped the bark of the tree tightly with his fingers.

The noise grew louder and louder... The sound of giant footsteps coming closer and closer and closer...

THUMP!

THUMP!

THUMP!

'**RAAAR!**'

Danny's heart beat so fast he thought it might explode.

What on earth was it?!

And then, between a pair of giant trees about 50 meters away, he saw it!

A creature so big, frightening and menacing that it made Danny's blood run cold in his veins. And yet it looked so very familiar. He'd seen many pictures of it in his books, but never in his wildest dreams had he ever thought that he'd ever see one in the flesh...

...a gigantic, ferocious, blood-thirsty... Tyrannosaurus rex!

Falling Into The Past

Danny couldn't believe what he was seeing. He gulped and rubbed his eyes.

This cannot be happening! Surely this was a dream - no, a nightmare!

Danny And The Dinosaurs

He opened his eyes again, but the T. rex was still there - as large as life! It was standing still now, steam snorting hard out of it's nostrils. Big, long, gusty bursts. And its head was darting around from side to side as if it was searching for something...

... Something to eat!

Danny gulped and he felt a shiver of fear shooting down his spine like ice. He crouched down lower against the tree, hoping the T. rex hadn't spotted him.

The dinosaur started to walk forwards again with slow, deliberate steps. The undergrowth crackled and crunched under the weight of its enormous, clawed feet.

Closer and closer it came, until it was just a few feet away from where Danny was hiding. He held his breath, not daring to make the slightest sound, and clung onto the bark even tighter.

The huge dinosaur stopped still in its tracks and sniffed the air. *SNIFF, SNIFF*, it went as it took in huge lungfuls of air through its nostrils.

It moved its head from side to side again, its huge piercing eyes searching the ground carefully. Then, suddenly, its head stopped. It sniffed again, quicker this time as if it had found a scent of something. Its head then swung quickly around and its eyes narrowed as it focused in on ... Danny!

'*Aaargh!*' screamed Danny as the T. rex lurched in his direction.

He jumped up from his hiding place and began running as fast as he had ever run in his entire life.

Falling Into The Past

In a flash, the huge dinosaur changed direction and began to give chase.

THUMP!

THUMP!

THUMP!

Danny ran and ran, weaving in and out of the trees in a desperate bid to escape. He jumped over fallen branches, darted around giant plants and scrambled through thick ferns. His legs were a whirl and his arms a blur as he hurtled through the forest at break-neck speed.

But still the T. rex followed!

THUMP!

THUMP!

THUMP!

'RAAAR!'

Danny dared not look back to see how close it was, but he could tell by how near its pounding feet sounded that it was right behind him, maybe no more than 30 meters away. Panting and gasping for air Danny ran on, desperately searching for a place to escape.

He darted around a fallen tree, but his foot became tangled in the loose branches and he crashed to the forest floor with a terrific thud. Desperately, he kicked himself free and began scrambling to his feet again. Behind him, the T. rex roared an almighty roar that rumbled in Danny's ears like thunder.

'RAAAR!'

It had now gained ground on him. As he stood up, Danny was facing right towards it. The T. rex was no more than 20 meters away! It snapped its great jaws at him hungrily and pounded relentlessly towards him, its eyes flashing cruel and merciless menace.

Danny yelled out in terror and began to run again, but as he did so a strange voice suddenly called out to him.

'Over here!' it cried.

Danny's eyes searched the forest.

'Quick!' cried the voice again.

And then Danny saw it - a small dinosaur waving frantically at him from behind a bush to his right.

Falling Into The Past

A talking dinosaur?!

'RAAAR!' boomed the T. rex again as it raced towards him.

No time to ask questions, thought Danny. And he dived into the bushes behind the small dinosaur.

'This way, hurry!' it cried and set off through the forest like a shot.

It ran as fast as lightning and Danny struggled to keep up as it wove along a small pathway between the trees.

'C'mon - keep moving!' the dinosaur urged, 'we're nearly there!'

But Danny was slowing down. He was utterly exhausted by now and he was breathing so hard he thought his lungs were going to burst. His legs, which had previously carried him so fast through the forest, were now aching all over and felt as if they were turning to jelly.

He couldn't go on much further, he just couldn't!

The T. rex was gaining on them. With every bound of its powerful legs it got closer and closer to Danny and the small dinosaur. Its huge roars shook the forest.

'RAAAR!'

THUMP!

THUMP!

THUMP!

It seemed to sense that its victory was near, like a lion just before it takes down an antelope.

But still Danny ran on, bravely ignoring the searing pains in his chest and summoning every ounce of his strength to keep his legs pumping forwards.

Danny And The Dinosaurs

In and out the trees they went, following the winding pathway until all of a sudden they came to an abrupt stop. Danny stumbled to a halt in shock.

He stared in disbelief. He couldn't believe what he was seeing.

A cliff edge! They were right in front of a cliff edge!

'Oops!' cried the small dinosaur. 'Wrong way!'

Oh my gosh! thought Danny. *What was he going to do, now?! He was doomed! There was nowhere to go! Was this a trick? Had the little dinosaur lured him here on purpose?*

Questions buzzed and whizzed around in Danny's head like confused bees. He quickly scampered forwards and peered over the edge of the cliff. *It was a very long way to the ground below. Was there a way to climb down? No, it didn't look like there was...*

'RAAAAAAR!'

Danny shot around and stared up in horror at the T. rex which was now standing just a few meters away. It was breathing heavily and the snorts of air coming out of its mouth sounded like a steam train.

Then, with slow deliberate steps, it began to move forward - its piercing eyes never leaving Danny for a second. Danny, trembling with fright, inched slowly backwards, nearer and nearer to the very edge of the cliff.

Then, with a flash of movement, the T. rex made its attack!

With a mighty roar it leapt into the air and dived at him, its enormous jaws snapping like ivory castanets. As Danny tried to scramble sideways out of the way, a pair of sharp talons suddenly grabbed him!

Dino Island

The wind rushed through Danny's ears as he felt himself being lifted from the ground. He shut his eyes in terror and a scream escaped his lips.

Oh no! He was going to be eaten alive by a hungry T. rex!

He desperately tried to squirm his way free, but the talons closed around him like an iron fist.

'*Heeeelp!*' he shouted into the wind.

'It's okay!' shouted another voice.

Danny opened his eyes again and spun his head around in the direction of the voice. The small dinosaur that had led him to the cliff dangled in the air beside him, its hands clasped tightly around a taloned foot.

Danny hesitated. *A taloned foot? But a T. rex wouldn't pick you up by its foot!*

He risked a glance upwards, terrified of being eaten. But instead of seeing the giant T. rex, all he could see were a set of great flapping wings!

'What's that?!' he called to the small dinosaur.

Danny And The Dinosaurs

'He's my friend, Rodak,' called back the dinosaur. 'He's a pterodactyl.'

Danny was so surprised he couldn't think of a reply.

'My name is Torp, what's yours?'

'Danny Trotter.'

'Very pleased to meet you Danny Trotter.'

'And you,' replied Danny.

The huge dinosaur bird swept up higher and higher into the air, its wings beating in long, powerful strokes. And as it did so, a great roar thundered up from below. Danny looked down to see the thwarted T. rex, standing at the edge of the cliff as it bellowed into the sky with frustration and anger. It had just lost its dinner!

'Phew! Your friend rescued us just in time!' shouted Danny over the roar of the wind.'

'You can always rely on Rodak! He's got me out of a few scrapes in the past.'

'Well, I'm glad he was around to help. He then paused before asking: 'Where on earth am I?'

'You're in Dino World, of course,' replied Torp.

'Dino World?'

'Yes.'

'And where is the pterodactyl taking us?'

The small dinosaur pointed to the North. 'To Dino Island - that's where I live.'

The great pterodactyl suddenly pushed forward with astonishing speed and Danny and Torp couldn't talk any more over the roar of the wind howling in their ears. The forest spooled out beneath them and soon they left it far behind.

Onwards they flew, over hills and mountains and valleys. It looked just like Africa did on those TV shows where they filmed it from the air. As Danny looked down, he could see huge herds of dinosaurs wandering all over the surface. There were hundreds of them!

Danny And The Dinosaurs

Some were absolutely huge, with immensely long necks and tails. *Brontosauruses!* thought Danny in excitement. *Or maybe they were diplodocuses?* They were too far away to tell.

Others were smaller, with 3 huge horns coming out from their heads. *Triceratops!* Danny gazed down in astonishment at all the different species of dinosaur he could see. Big dinosaurs, small dinosaurs, horned dinosaurs, thin dinosaurs, tall dinosaurs. He recognized many of them from his picture books, but there were lots he didn't recognize or they were just too far away to get a really good look at.

Soon they were approaching a vast river which cut through the breathtaking landscape like a silver ribbon of sparkling crystal. Located right in the middle was a large island, and this is where the pterodactyl seemed to be heading.

From high up in the sky, Danny could see it contained mountain ranges, forests and sweeping hills and valleys. There was also an immense grassy plain which stretched far and wide into the distance.

As they flew on, Danny couldn't help but feel he was somehow in a dream. *It was incredible! Here he was, flying above a world populated by dinosaurs. Real, live, dinosaurs!*

He could hardly believe it!

Danny was still marveling at it all when he realized that they were now starting to descend steadily towards the island. Lower and lower they went. Finally, with a curving sweep, the pterodactyl flew low over a sweeping hillside and glided over the giant plain of grassland filled with dozens and dozens of huge dinosaurs quietly grazing.

Just before the pterodactyl landed, it let Danny and Torp drop softly to the ground.

'Thanks, Rodak!' said Torp as he jumped to his feet.

The pterodactyl landed on the ground close by and closed its giant wings against its body. It then stood there, eyeing him coolly.

'Thanking me is all well and good, young Torp. But this isn't the first time I've had to come to your rescue, is it?'

Torp nodded, sheepishly.

'This must be the fifth time this month I've helped you out of some scrape you've gotten yourself into. Really, this is getting to be a bit much!'

'Sorry, Rodak.'

'Yes, well, I should think so!' said the pterodactyl , adopting a rather haughty air. He puffed out his chest a little. 'I'll have you know that I've far more important things to be doing with my time than rescuing you and your new friend from some no-good T. rex.'

'It won't happen again, I promise!'

'I find that hard to believe,' replied the pterodactyl curtly. 'And how on earth did you get to the Dark Forest anyway? Its on the mainland, miles and miles from here.'

'I hitched a ride from Graarg the pterosaur,' replied Torp brightly. 'He was flying to Volcano Mountain for the summer and didn't mind dropping me off on the way.'

'And *how*, pray tell, did you intend to get back home?' said Rodak.

'Er… well I hadn't thought about that.'

'That doesn't surprise me at all,' said Rodak in an exasperated tone. 'And what on earth were you doing in the Dark Forest, anyway?'

'Exploring. The Dark Forest is far more interesting than the grassy plains. But then I saw Danny being chased by one of those horrible T. rex and I thought he could use some help. So I thought I'd take him to the limestone caves to hide. Only, I kind of took the wrong turning and we ended up at the edge of that cliff.'

'We're terribly grateful for your help,' said Danny. 'If it hadn't been for you then we'd have ended up as that dinosaur's dinner.'

'I have no doubt about it,' replied Rodak matter-of-factly. 'Those T. rex in the Dark Forest only ever think of one thing - food! Terribly vulgar and rude they are too, by the way. No manners at all. So, it was a very good job for you two that I was flying overhead at just the right time and spotted you.'

'Thank you very much for rescuing us,' said Danny.

'Well, I hope it's the *last* time I have to do so. I'm a very busy and important dinosaur, I'll have you know. Now, time is getting on. I have lots of urgent and very important things I need to be attending to.'

And with that, he opened his great wings out from the sides of his body and began running along the thick grass. In a few seconds he was up in the air again and flying high into the sunlit sky.

Dino Island

Danny watched as the dinosaur soared higher and higher, eventually dissolving into a small speck in the far distance, framed by the puffy white clouds.

When he looked back down again, Danny found himself surrounded by a small group of dinosaurs that had wandered over from where they had been grazing.

Danny And The Dinosaurs

Amongst them was a T. rex, almost as tall as the one he had just escaped from in the forest. Danny gasped and jumped back in panic.

'Run!' he yelled.

He sprung forward, as if to get away, but Torp's hand snaked out and took him by the shoulder.

'It's okay,' he said, smiling. 'These are my friends.'

'B-but that's a T. rex!' Danny exclaimed.

'Yes, but he's not like the other T. rex in Dino World. We're different here on Dino Island. No one will hurt you.'

The dinosaurs had edged forward to gawk at the newcomer. Their whispers rustled through the air like leaves in the wind. The T. rex, a large and weathered old dinosaur, stepped forward out of the crowd.

'So, who is this human you've brought to our home?' he asked Torp.

Danny could see the old dinosaur wasn't best pleased with Torp for bringing him to their land.

Torp hopped from foot to foot. 'But I *had* to bring him! He was being chased by one of those horrible, stupid Tyrannosaurs in the Dark Forest. If I hadn't have tried to save him, then he'd have been eaten for sure!'

The old dinosaur looked at Danny cautiously. 'Is this true, young man?'

Danny nodded, unable to talk.

'Well then,' said the old dinosaur adopting a more friendly tone, 'my name is Brintus and I am the leader of the dinosaurs in this part of our world. Welcome to Dino Island.'

'Um, thank you,' replied Danny nervously. 'My name is Danny Trotter. But why aren't you all fierce and ferocious like that other T. rex that tried to gobble me up for its dinner?'

The dinosaur smiled. 'We aren't *all* like that, you know. The Tyrannosaurus that live in the Dark Forest come from a different herd than me. They are very primitive, stupid and unpleasant. They haven't even learned to talk yet. Mind you, only us dinosaurs living here on Dino Island can talk.'

'How come?'

'I don't really know. It's always been that way.'

Another dinosaur stepped forward. It arched its long neck downwards and blinked at Danny.

'Hello, Danny, I'm Molvus.'

'You're a brontosaurus!' Danny grinned.

'Why, yes. As a matter of fact, I am. How on earth did you know that?'

'I've got lots of books on dinosaurs at home, with pictures and everything!'

'Well, I never!' replied Molvus looking rather surprised.

Another dinosaur came forward, who just happened to be a female dinosaur. 'A very good day to you, young Danny,' she said batting her thick eyelashes. 'My name is Israd.'

'You're a stegosaurus!'

'Ooh, isn't he clever?!' she replied, looking around at the other dinosaurs. They all nodded in agreement. 'As you may probably have noticed,' Israd continued, 'I'm the most beautiful dinosaur on the whole island.'

Danny giggled. *A vain dinosaur - whatever next!*

After the rest of the dinosaurs had introduced themselves to Danny, Brintus said: 'Why don't you come with me and we can have a talk about how you got here?'

The dinosaur led Danny over to a clear space away from the group and asked Danny to take a seat in the grass.

When Danny had made himself comfortable, Brintus continued: 'You may have sensed that I was a little suspicious of you when Torp first introduced you.'

'Yes, I kinda got that feeling,' replied Danny.

'Well, that was because you are not the first human creature to visit our land.'

'Really?!'

'Indeed. There has been another - a very nasty and unpleasant individual. But I can see that you are not evil like him.'

'Who is he?'

'Never mind about him for the time being, Danny. First, I would like to know how you got here.'

'Well, it's a very strange story...' began Danny.

Brintus listened quietly as Danny told him all that had happened. He told the dinosaur all about his Uncle Felix, the mysterious egg, how he had cleaned it with the *Time Travel Night Cream* he'd found in the bathroom cabinet and how the egg had suddenly grown in size.

Danny carefully described everything that had occurred, right up to the point when Rodak had dropped him and Torp onto the vast, grassy plain of Dino Island.

When he had finished, Danny gazed up into Brintus's eyes, wondering what the old dinosaur would make of the extraordinary tale he had just been told. Danny figured that Brintus wouldn't even understand most of what he'd said. After all, things like houses, bathroom cabinets and skin cream hadn't even been invented yet. He couldn't expect a dinosaur to have a clue what they were. But the dinosaur didn't seem confused or bewildered at all.

Strange, thought Danny. *Brintus seems to understand everything. But perhaps he shouldn't be so surprised. After all, the dinosaurs could speak English!*

Danny gave up trying to work out how the dinosaur seemed to know about modern life. He had thought of asking, but now didn't seem to be the right time to do it.

For a few moments Brintus stared blankly ahead, his mind deeply lost in thought.

Eventually he said, 'What color did you say the egg was?'

Danny scratched his head. 'Oh, I forgot to say! It was green. The deepest, most extraordinary shade of green I have ever seen. And once, when I was first looking at it at Uncle Felix's house, the color seemed to move and float over the surface like syrup!'

Slowly, the dinosaur's eyes gradually began to light up and twinkle.

The wise old dinosaur gave Danny a knowing look and a faint smile appeared at the corners of his mouth.

'Ah,' said Brintus. '*That* explains how you got here!'

'What do you mean?'

'Well, that certainly wasn't a dinosaur's egg your uncle found.'

Danny looked at him with a puzzled face. 'Wasn't it? Well, what on earth was it, then?'

'It was a dragon's egg.'

Danny's mouth widened in surprise. 'A dragon's egg?! But I didn't think dragons even existed.'

'Oh, yes, they most certainly do,' replied Brintus firmly. 'They live right here on this island in a place called Dragon Realm.' He pointed towards a group of high mountains which could be seen in the far off distance. 'That's it, over there. So you see, dragons are as real as you or I.'

'That's amazing!' replied Danny.

'Dragons are very magical creatures, you know,' continued Brintus, 'and so are their eggs. The liquid you used to clean your egg with must have awakened its magic somehow and that's how it transported you here to Dino World.'

'But that means that when I fell into the egg I must have traveled back in time millions and millions of years!'

'Well, yes - I guess so,' Brintus shrugged.

Danny rocked back on his heels and gazed at Brintus in wonder. 'Wow!' he said, because there were no words big enough to capture how he felt.

Danny Volunteers To Help

For some moments Danny and Brintus remained silent. The only sounds to be heard were the gentle rustling of the grass and the buzzing of giant insects as they darted and weaved through the humid air.

The strong smell of pollen drifted lazily about in the wind.

Everything looked so peaceful here on Dino Island, thought Danny. And it certainly was a beautiful place. The grassy plain, stretching out before him like a soft carpet of shimmering green, was bordered by colossal trees that stretched high into the sky like gigantic wooden skyscrapers.

In the far distance, towering mountain ranges could be seen, their snow-capped peaks glinting in the light of the sun which hung in the sky like a giant sphere of golden honey. Further to the left lay a group of volcanoes, their flaming red peaks sparkling like fire-works through billowy clouds of silvery smoke.

The sky was a dazzling shade of orangey blue and the air smelt so fresh and clean - so unlike the polluted air from home. And how wonderful to be able to see all these dinosaurs up close. Danny used to think they would be frightening since they were so big, but apart from the scary T. rex in the forest, they all seemed very friendly.

He pulled a handful of grass from the ground, then dropped it and let the breeze carry it gently away into the air.

'This is a very beautiful place,' he said, looking up at Brintus. 'I bet you love living here.'

The old dinosaur paused for a second before replying, 'Yes, Dino Island is a wonderful home, but...' His voice then dropped off into silence and he gazed down sadly at the ground.

'But, what?' asked Danny.

'We may not be able to live here for much longer.'

'Why on earth not?'

'Remember I mentioned earlier that there was another human in Dino World?'

'Yes, who is he?'

'His name is Professor Zoran, a very cruel and evil man. He arrived in Dino World some time ago and then traveled here to Dino Island. At first he was very friendly, explaining that he had traveled back in time from the future and all he wanted to do was study and examine us for his work. So we let him. He measured us, took photographs of us and performed all kinds of studies. We didn't mind at all.

'But then one day, he just vanished. He was nowhere to be seen. The hut he had been living in was totally empty and there was no sign of him anywhere else. Not on the grass plain, or the hillsides or near the river.'

'That is quite mysterious,' said Danny.

'Indeed it was,' agreed Brintus nodding his huge head. 'Anyway, some days later we all heard some very strange sounds coming from the Great Forest. Our hearing is very good, you know. So even though the Great Forest is a long way away, the sounds were unmistakable: Loud banging noises, whirring sounds, crashes and the sound of yelling.'

'What could it be?' Danny asked.

'Well, that's what we wanted to know,' replied Brintus, 'so Rodak flew over the Great Forest to try and find out what the cause of all this great hullabaloo was. And do you know what he saw?'

'No. What did he see?'

'He saw a big castle being built in the forest. The place was like a great big building site, full of diggers and cranes and scaffolding everywhere. And huge blocks of granite were being put into place by a small army of men. And there, in the middle of all this, was Professor Zoran ordering these men about and telling them what to do.'

'Did Rodak see anything else?'

'Oh, yes. And this was the most disturbing thing. It was what alerted us to the fact that Professor Zoran wasn't all that he seemed. He wasn't the friendly person we had first thought him to be.'

'What was it?'

'On the far side of the castle was a gigantic cage.'

'A cage?!'

'Yes. And do you know what was in the cage?'

'No - please tell me.'

'A dragon.'

'A dragon?! Danny's mouth opened wide in surprise.

'Yes. I told you they were real, didn't I? But this was not any old dragon, mind you. It was the Great Dragon Draco, who has reigned over this land for hundreds and hundreds of years.'

'But what was he doing in the cage?'

'Well, that's what Rodak wanted to know. So he glided down very quietly so that none of the work men or Professor Zoran would see him and landed near the huge cage that Draco the dragon was imprisoned in. And that is when Draco told him all about the castle and Professor Zoran's evil plans.'

'Does the castle have a name?'

'Yes. Draco said that Professor Zoran had named it Evilstone Castle.'

'Ugh! What a creepy name!' said Danny. 'And what are the professor's plans?'

'Draco explained that Professor Zoran had captured him so that he could collect his tears.'

'Collect his tears? What on earth would the professor want with a dragon's tears?'

Danny Volunteers To Help

'Remember, young Danny, that I told you that dragons are very magical creatures?'

'Yes, I remember.'

'Well then, the tears of a dragon have very special and immensely powerful magic contained in them. There is perhaps nothing quite as powerful as dragon's tears - not even the horn of a unicorn.'

'So Professor Zoran is going to use the dragon's tears for a magic spell?'

'Yes, that is correct. Draco the dragon explained that the professor intends to build a gigantic zoo next to his castle. The cage he was in was just the first of many such cages that were going to be built.'

'And what was he going to put in all the other cages?'

'Us!'

'What?!' gasped Danny in surprise. 'That would be awful. Why would anyone want to put such amazing creatures inside cages?'

'Well, I'm afraid it's true, young Danny. Professor Zoran intends to put the dinosaurs of Dino Island in his gigantic zoo. We will all go in cages and there we will stay, imprisoned for the rest of our lives.'

'But why does he want to put you in a zoo?

'He intends to charge very rich human beings a lot of money to take them back in time to Dino Island and see the dinosaurs in his zoo.'

'But why doesn't he just capture the dinosaurs roaming around in the Great Forest? He wouldn't need to build a magic bridge, then.'

'They can't talk like we can. Apparently, human beings will pay even more money to visit a zoo with *talking* dinosaurs.'

'That's terrible,' said Danny sadly. He gazed down at the ground thoughtfully, feeling rather ashamed of his fellow humans.

'Dinosaurs don't belong in a zoo,' he continued, but I still don't understand why Professor Zoran needs the dragon's tears.'

'Well, separating the Great Forest from where we are now is the Great River. The professor has no way to transport us across.'

'Can't he use a boat?'

'The river-dwelling dinosaurs would capsize it and gobble him up as soon as he set sail over here.'

'What about a bridge?'

'The river is far too wide for a *normal* bridge. That's why he needs the dragon's tears. 10 gallons of them - according to Draco.'

'So he can build a *magical* bridge!' exclaimed Danny.'

'That is correct, young Danny. Only a magical bridge would be able to stretch wide enough to span the Great River. And only the tears from a dragon have powerful enough magic to build such a long and mighty bridge.'

'This is terrible,' said Danny. 'But how on earth did Professor Zoran manage to catch a dragon?'

Brintus shook his head. 'I wish I knew. Before Draco the dragon could explain any more, one of Professor Zoran's guards spotted them talking and opened fire on Rodak with a gun. He only just managed to escape with his life. All this happened quite a long time ago.

'But what about the zoo?'

'That has now been completed. Rodak flew over the castle just recently. According to him, there are now hundreds and hundreds of gigantic cages sitting out there in the forest, just waiting for an unfortunate dinosaur.'

'Was Draco still there in his cage?'

'No. There was no sign of him at all. Professor Zoran must have moved him into his castle to hide him away from prying eyes.'

'But if Draco has magical powers, why doesn't he use them to free himself?'

'That is quite a mystery, young Danny - we just don't know.'

'But surely there is something you can do to stop Professor Zoran?'

'The only way to stop him is to rescue Draco before the professor gathers the ten gallons of tears he needs for his magical spell. Dragons can only cry a few tears a day, but Draco has been imprisoned for a very long time now. Professor Zoran could reach the required amount any day now, and when he does that, he'll have enough magic to build the bridge and capture us all.'

'Why don't you try rescuing Draco?' asked Danny.

Brintus swished his long tail. 'The Great Forest is very dense in places - the trees grow very close together. Large dinosaurs like me are too big to get through. And we are also too big to get into Evilstone Castle. And besides, it is guarded by Professor Zoran' guards who all have guns. They would see us coming and we'd never get close enough to free Draco.'

Danny thought carefully about the whole situation. Then an idea suddenly came in to his head.

'What about me?!' he exclaimed. 'I'm only small! I could easily get through the dense part of the forest and sneak into the castle.'

Brintus frowned in thought. 'No, no… we couldn't expect you to try something so dangerous on our behalf.'

'But it's the only way to save Draco,' pointed out Danny. 'I'll be OK. I'm fast and quick and very good at hiding - they won't catch me.'

Brintus hesitated for a moment before saying, 'You are a very brave young man Danny. But you cannot go on your own.'

Danny's mind thrilled with different emotions. He was scared and unsure, but most of all he was angry that someone would want to treat the dinosaurs so badly.

'I can bring Torp with me,' he said. 'He's only a small dinosaur.'

'Hmmm, he may be small but he's very young and impulsive. If I do let you go, then I think Israd should escort you to the castle in order to keep an eye on you both. She isn't as huge as dinosaurs like me, so she'll be able to get through the dense forest quite easily.'

'Great!' cried Danny. 'Oh, please let me go. I'm sure I can rescue Draco!'

Danny Volunteers To Help

Brintus lapsed into silence once more as he thought long and hard about the idea.

While he thought there may be great danger, there was just no other way to save the great dragon Draco and the dinosaurs in Dino Island. If Danny didn't go, then they would all be surely doomed to spend the rest of their lives in cages in Professor Zoran's monstrous zoo...

'Very well then' he said. 'Let's do it!'

Mission Impossible?

Although Danny had agreed to help the dinosaurs, he couldn't help but feel a little kernel of fear rolling around in his stomach.

What if he got caught? What if the evil Professor Zoran caught him and put him in the zoo as well? He shuddered at the thought. But he couldn't refuse to help the dinosaurs, he just couldn't. What the professor was doing was so wrong that it made Danny's blood boil.

'Let's tell the others about your plan,' said Brintus.

They slowly walked back across the great plain, the grass swaying all around them, and headed through the throng of dinosaurs. Most of them kept eating but Danny could feel their wary eyes on him. He had a lot to prove to the dinosaurs. Their experiences of humans hadn't been very good so far.

Brintus gathered all the dinosaurs together and then carefully explained all about Danny's plan to rescue Draco the dragon. When he had finished, he looked around to see what their reaction was.

Danny And The Dinosaurs

Torp, unsurprisingly, was the first to respond. 'What a great plan!' he cried enthusiastically. 'I can't wait to get to Evilstone Castle and give Professor Zoran a good bashing! I'm not afraid of that brute. I'll belt him on the nose! I'll box his ears! I'll punch his lights out, I'll…'

'Now, now, Torp,' interrupted Brintus sternly, 'that's enough of that! We'll have no talk of violence. Violence is wrong. You are going there to save Draco and that is all.'

Torp looked down at the grass sheepishly. He then paused in thought for a moment before asking hopefully: 'Couldn't I at least kick his butt?'

'No!' replied Brintus firmly.

'Well, I think it is a simply wonderful idea,' said Israd as she batted her eyelashes excitedly. 'We simply must save dear old Draco from that horrible Professor Zoran. What a completely ghastly man! I'll most certainly accompany Danny through the forest - as long as I'm able to get back for bed time. I do need my beauty sleep, you know!'

'I think it is an excellent plan,' said a triceratops from the back of the group. 'It is rather dangerous, but if this brave boy is willing to try then I say good luck to him.'

'Me too!' said a diplodocus.

'And me!' said a large brachiosaurus, munching on a green cycad plant.

'Three cheers for Danny!' cried an iguanodon.

'Hey, what about me? I'm going too!' said Torp indignantly.

Everybody burst out laughing.

Mission Impossible?

'So I take it that everyone agrees that Danny's plan is worth trying?' said Brintus when the laughter had died down. Every dinosaur in the large group nodded their heads in agreement.

There was no time to waste. Danny, Torp and Israd immediately began preparing themselves for their long and dangerous journey.

As Danny got himself ready, Brintus came up to him, leaned down and handed him a very strange object. Danny held it in the palm of his open hand and peered down at it. The object was about as big as a Coke bottle and was long and curvy and had jagged edges down part of one side. It was also dazzlingly white.

'What is it?' asked Danny.

'It's a dragon's tooth,' said Brintus softly. 'Rodak found it on the outskirts of the Great Forest. He was flying back one day, after spying on Evilstone Castle, when his eagle eyes spotted it on the ground, lying at the bottom of a steep hill. So he swooped down and picked it up.'

'But why? What's so special about a dragon's tooth?'

'Brintus smiled. 'You have much to learn about Dino Island, young Danny. A dragon's tooth contains a special kind of magic. With its powers, the one who holds it in their hand is granted three wishes.'

'Really?'

'Yes. We have kept the tooth safe, ready to use when the need arises. Well, this is just such a time. So I give the tooth to you, Danny. It is now yours. Guard it well.'

'I will. I promise!' said Danny.

'If you get into trouble you can use it to help you out,' said Brintus. 'In times of danger, just hold it next to your heart, make a wish and then rub it with your hand. But it can only protect *you* Danny, and it only has enough magic in it for three wishes. So use them well, young human. Use them well…'

Danny stared at the precious gift in awe.

WOW! A magic dragon's tooth! he thought before slipping it safely into his pocket. 'Thank you, Brintus,' he said. 'I won't let you down.'

The three intrepid travelers were finally ready. They had been given the directions to Evilstone Castle and now had a firm grasp of how to get there.

First, they were to travel to the north easterly tip of Dino Island, where the land jutted out the furthest into the waters of the Great River. This way, their journey across the treacherous expanse wouldn't be so far. Once across the Great River, they would then travel south through the Great Forest towards Evilstone Castle.

With everyone gathered around again, Brintus made a small speech to the assembled group.

'Fellow dinosaurs of Dino Island - and our new friend young Danny - these are dark times for us all. Our freedom and our liberty are in great peril. As you all know, the evil Professor Zoran intends to capture us all and imprison us in the zoo he has built next to his castle in the Great Forest.

Mission Impossible?

'And to this end, he has made our great friend Draco the dragon his prisoner in order to collect enough tears for his spell. A spell that will enable him to build a mighty bridge over the Great River that will enable Professor Zoran to transport us back to his zoo.

'But in these dark days a tiny ray of hope has appeared in the form of a small boy from a land and time far, far away. While he may be small in size, his heart is as big and brave as the largest giant's. This young boy does not have to help us, he owes us no allegiance whatsoever. But with his brave heart comes his compassion and his understanding of what is just and what is right. He is prepared to fight for these noble values, in spite of any personal danger to himself. And for that we most truly thank him.

'So good luck on your journey, young Danny. And good luck to you too, Israd and Torp. The future of us all depends on you. May justice be triumphant in your perilous quest!'

A great cheer sprang up so loud that Danny had to cover his ears from the noise. But he was greatly touched and honored by Brintus's words and as he made his way through the crowd of dinosaurs he felt ten feet tall.

Israd was waiting patiently for him in the cool shade beneath a giant ginkgo tree.

'Hop aboard, young Danny!' she said as she saw him approaching. 'You can ride on my back and hold on to the beautiful protective plates that are there. Aren't they lovely and pretty?'

Danny And The Dinosaurs

'Yes, they are.' Danny grinned as he climbed on to the stegosaurus' back. The Stegosaurus' skin was rough and bumpy, but not in any way uncomfortable. He carefully positioned himself between four large, bony plates and held onto the two in front of him with each hand.

Just then a scampering sound could be heard and Danny looked round to see Torp scurrying towards them.

'Wait for me, wait for me!' he cried excitedly. 'We're off on a dangerous and perilous mission to rescue a dragon! And when we meet that horrible Professor Zoran he's going to get what's coming to him. Oh, yes! I'll bash him and biff him and whop him and…'

'*Torp!*' said Brintus gravely. 'What did I tell you?'

'Yeah, yeah, OK…' replied Torp feeling the full force of the old dinosaur's stare.

Danny giggled. He knew that Torp wouldn't really hurt Professor Zoran, it was all just talk and bravado. He guessed that Brintus knew this perfectly well, too.

'Are you sitting comfortably, young Danny?' asked Israd.

'Yes, thank you,' he replied.

'What are we waiting for?! cried Torp. 'I'm not scared of any danger, the more the better I say! There's nothing that can scare me! Off we go, off we go - there's no time to lose!'

Mission Impossible?

And with that, they set off at a run towards the Great Forest.

'Good luck to all of you!' cried Brintus's voice be-hind them as they left. 'Good luck to you all…'

71

The Great River

Israd ran and ran, her bulky legs pounding quickly over the open plain.

Danny gripped hard onto the two bony plates in front of him as he was vigorously jostled up and down.

He found the ride uncomfortable at first, but once he became accustomed to the movement of Israd as she bounded forwards he started to move his body in rhythm to hers. This made things a lot smoother and he began to relax a little and actually started to enjoy the ride.

Torp darted on up ahead, his nimble feet effortlessly gliding over the ground with ease.

As they traveled on their journey, Danny gazed around in wonder at the astonishing scenery of this extraordinary, prehistoric world.

The grass they were traveling over was much thicker and courser than the grass back home and every so often they would pass giant plants with strange looking silver and reddish leaves which were as big as car tires.

Danny And The Dinosaurs

Fern trees swayed gently to and fro in the warm breeze, bizarre looking insects the size of birds busily flitting around their green foliage.

Even the sky appeared different. It had a mysterious, orangey glow to it and Danny wondered if this was because of all the volcanoes that dotted the landscape, spewing out great clouds of fiery smoke like ancient chimneys.

Time passed, and eventually the grassy plain gave way to a more rocky and hilly terrain. The three travelers soon found themselves slowing down as they had to carefully navigate their way up between huge boulders and harsh, jagged rocks as they climbed their way upwards.

Onwards they went, higher and higher. The climb was steep, but they kept going until they reached a large opening between the rocks, situated right at the very top of the hill. They passed through to the other side and then made the slow journey down, having to maneuver themselves around even more boulders and rocky debris.

Once they were down again the rocky surface eventually dissolved into another grass plain and their progress resumed at its earlier speed.

On and on they continued over the beautiful landscape of Dino Island.

Through woods and thickets, over great valleys and hills - they never stopped for even a moment, until the sky slowly darkened into late afternoon.

Finally, as a cloud lazily slunk itself across the face of the glowing sun, Danny spotted what he thought was a river in the far off distance. He could just make out tiny slivers of twinkling light, ebbing and flowing gently as they threw out shimmering sparks of golden brightness which winked in and out of existence like ghosts.

'Hey, is that the Great River up ahead?' he asked, excitement rising in his voice.

'Indeed it is my dear boy... indeed it is! replied Israd, slightly panting from the effort of running. She had now been traveling for several hours and was getting very tired.

'I'll be ever so glad when we reach the river,' she continued, 'so that I can dip my poor aching feet into that lovely, cool water. They feel like they're about to drop off my legs at any minute!'

'This is no time to be worrying about your smelly feet!' cried Torp who was still running a few yards up ahead. 'We've got a top secret, highly dangerous mission to accomplish, remember? We need to push on and get to Professor Zoran's castle as soon as possible - we haven't got time to wait around while you go paddling about in the water.'

'Young Torp,' replied Israd, sternly, 'when you get to my great age you may realize that impatience can cause the wisest of dinosaurs to do the most foolish of things. I am a lot older than you and my poor old feet need a rest. If they don't, then I shall be in no fit condition to travel through the Great Forest. And then where'd we be, *hmmm?*'

'She's right, you know.' said Danny. 'Water is very good for tired and swollen feet.'

'Hey, whose side are you on?' cried Torp. 'I thought us young ones stuck together?'

'And my feet *aren't* smelly!' insisted Israd. 'I'll have you know that I bathe them in the rich, cleansing sap of the Calamite tree every Monday and Wednesday afternoons.'

'Well, you better bathe them on Tuesday and Thursday afternoons as well because I can smell them from here!' replied Torp with a grin.

'Oh, you cheeky young scamp!' exclaimed Israd indignantly.

And so their journey continued, leading them closer and closer to the Great River that slowly began to open out before them in a rich tapestry of rippling silver waves and sparkling white foam.

Finally, as the sun sunk ever lower towards the orange tinted horizon, they reached the shoreline of the biggest and widest river that Danny had ever seen. The crystal clear water gently lapped against the sandy bank and Danny couldn't help feeling breathless with wonder as he gazed across the vast expanse of water stretching out in front of him, serene and tranquil in its liquid wonder. It seemed to go on for miles!

'Wow, no wonder it's called the *Great* River,' he said. 'It's the widest thing I've ever seen!' He stared across to the opposite side and squinted his eyes. It was so far away that it appeared quite difficult to make out clearly.

He could also see the Great Forest lying some distance farther back, the huge trees towering upwards towards the sky, a canopy of green covering their peaks like a blanket.

High above the trees, soaring majestically and effortlessly amongst the white, pillow-like clouds, was a small flock of pterodactyls. At least Danny guessed they were pterodactyls - they were too far away to be sure.

He carefully climbed down from Israd's back and stretched his legs. After several hours traveling in the same position they were quite stiff.

The Stegosaurus heaved her huge body down the slope of the sandy river bank, careful not to go too fast and lose her footing. When she reached the shoreline she slowly placed her right foot into the water and patted it down into the river bed below to see if it would hold her weight. Satisfied, she then placed her left foot forward and slowly walked into the sparkling water.

'Ooohhh, that's better!' She sighed, a smile of satisfaction crossing her face. 'What a relief! I don't think I could have gone on much longer, you know. I'm not used to all this running and gallivanting about.'

She began to paddle about in the water, swishing her legs to and fro and letting the refreshing crystal water gush soothingly between her tired and swollen toes.

Danny sat down next to Torp on a mound of thick grass and looked up into the sky. 'It will be getting dark, soon,' he said.

'Yes, that's why we need to cross the river before night fall,' replied Torp. 'Otherwise we won't be able to see where the other side of the river is. We don't want to end up swimming round and round in circles for hours.'

'That wouldn't be good at all,' agreed Danny.

They both lapsed into a thoughtful silence, the only sounds were the soft splish splosh of Israd's feet and the gentle humming of the ever-present insects as they buzzed around in the drifting breeze.

Finally, Israd emerged out of the water and plodded up the river bank to join Danny and Torp. 'Now then, dear friends,' she said brightly, 'I feel so much better now, I really do! My feet feel as right as rain. As clean as a whistle! As pretty as a picture!'

She gave them a beaming smile and did a little jig to demonstrate.

'Can we get going now, then?' asked Torp eagerly.

'Why, of course we can.' Israd beamed, fluttering her eyes happily. 'Now then, young Danny, hop onto my back again and cling on really, really tight. We're going into the river now and the water may get a little bit choppy.'

Danny did as he was told and once he was safely sitting on Israd's back the big dinosaur made her way down to the river once more and waddled slowly into the clear, bright water.

'Get a hold of my tail Torp,' she called out behind her, 'and hold on tight dear boy, hold on tight!'

Danny gulped nervously. *It was an awfully long way across to the other side. What if something went wrong? What*

The Great River

if Israd got tired again and couldn't go on? What if they were attacked by prehistoric crocodiles and eaten for dinner?

Be brave, Danny told himself. *Israd would look after him. She wouldn't let any harm come to him or Torp.*

The big dinosaur continued to wade further away from the shoreline and deeper and deeper into the icy waters of the Great River. As Israd's huge body sank further and further down into the river, Danny became worried that she would submerge completely and he would have to start swimming himself!

But he needn't have worried. Once the water had reached about three-quarters of the way up the dinosaur's body it remained there, a few meters below Danny's feet.

He breathed a sigh of relief and gripped hard onto the two bony plates in front of him. He glanced over his shoulder to make sure Torp was okay and was relieved to see the little dinosaur behind them, holding tightly onto Israd's long tail.

The next part of their journey was now underway, as they began the epic swim across the Great River which stretched out ahead of them like a vast and mighty ocean.

At first the water was quite calm and placid, but once they had ventured further out the waves became bigger and more forceful as they began to meet the strong river current which was flowing against the side of Israd's body

'Hang on my dears, hang on!' cried Israd encouragingly. 'I'm putting on a bit of a spurt now and we'll be over the other side in no time at all - you wait and see!'

Danny And The Dinosaurs

'Are you alright Torp?' called Danny, glancing backwards again.

'Sure am!' yelled the little dinosaur, brightly. 'And if any monsters come out of the water and attack us then just leave them to me! I'll bash them on the nose and box their ears and have their guts for garters. They won't know whether they're coming or going when I've finished with them!'

Danny certainly hoped that there weren't any monsters lurking menacingly beneath the water. He glanced down apprehensively as Israd swam onwards, her powerful legs churning and thrusting through the deep and flowing water.

He gripped more tightly to the thick plates on her back and made a little wish that all would be well.

On and on Israd swam, cutting through the water like a tug boat. And slowly but surely, the three intrepid travelers crossed the gigantic river.

Time passed... The sun dipped ever lower towards the darkening horizon... The wind continued to gently blow its whistling song past their ears... The clouds above floated across the skies like giant marshmallows...

They reached half way across the river... then three quarters of the way across...

And still Israd swam. She swam and she swam and she swam.

Eventually the welcoming sight of the river bank was within reach. Danny began to relax. Everything was going to be alright, he thought to himself. Within a couple of minutes they would reach the safety of the shoreline.

The Great River

He even allowed himself a little smile of relief. His fears about underwater beasts suddenly bursting out of the water and gobbling them up were completely groundless.

And then it appeared from below!

The Monster From The Deep

No one noticed it at first. The only visible sign of its presence was a small rectangle of scaly dark skin that protruded slightly out of the water.

The creature continued to track the three travelers. It moved swiftly and silently through the icy water, about twenty meters behind them. Its giant tail, (over five meters long) thrust back and forth effortlessly, propelling it through the water like a torpedo.

Its enormous head, (as big as an entire human adult) moved from side to side as it swam, and it opened and closed its massive jaws eagerly in anticipation of the meal to come. One hundred and thirty two thick, razor-sharp teeth gnashed together - each one as big as a railroad spike!

Now, you may be forgiven for thinking that this grotesque and frightening creature was an alligator, but you would be wrong. It was a lot bigger, meaner and a whole lot nastier than a mere crocodile!

For the hideous brute of a beast that was now closing in on the three travelers was none other than a sarcosuchus imperator, a distant relative of the crocodile that lived millions of years before the crocodiles we know today even existed.

This particular sarcosuchus was almost twice as long as the biggest alligator you could ever see today. As long, in fact, as a city bus! And it weighed about 10 tons. That's 10 tons of savage, unpleasant and exceedingly hungry sarcosuchus.

And it was getting closer…

… And closer…

'Only a short distance to go now, Israd,' said Danny excitedly. 'We're nearly there, keep going!'

'I will, dear, I will,' replied Israd wearily, 'but I'm ever so tired, you know. I feel like I've crossed three oceans and then gone back again for second helpings!'

'How are you doing back there?' Danny said as he turned his back towards Torp.

Then he saw it…

Two huge green reptilian eyes suddenly poked out of the water about 10 meters behind Torp. Danny didn't even hear the little dinosaur's reply. He just froze in shock.

The two green eyes blinked back at him, coldly. And then they rose further out of the water as a pair of massively long jaws emerged from beneath the surface, stretching out in front like a thick and bulky tree trunk.

The Monster From The Deep

Soon the creature's entire upper body was protruding out of the water as it made its race towards them. It had patiently bided its time, carefully stalking them and getting as close as it could before it could be detected.

Now it was time to make its strike!

Its tail lashed furiously from side to side, its powerful legs vigorously pushing one way and another, steering it accurately towards its prey. The water gushed and gurgled around its writhing body as it bolted forwards, sending bubbles of foamy spray violently up into the air above.

Torp glanced behind him to see what all the commotion was.

'Arrrgh!' he hollered as he caught site of the mighty sarcosuchus. 'A river monster!'

'Swim faster, Israd!' urged Danny as he finally found his voice again. 'There's a giant dinosaur beast behind us and it looks very hungry!'

'Oh, goodness gracious me!' cried Israd anxiously. 'And everything was going so well, too!'

She mustered every ounce of her strength and forced her tired and aching body to swim faster, frantically pushing herself onwards as she desperately made for the river bank ahead. Her legs furiously attacked the water, moving backwards and forwards in quick, rapid movements as she accelerated herself through the waves.

'Arrrgh! 'A river monster!' repeated Torp.

'Hurry, Israd, hurry!' yelled Danny. He looked around again at the ferocious and blood-thirsty predator behind them and gasped in horror.

It was gaining on them!

'It's getting closer!' cried Danny, frantically. 'Faster, Israd, faster!'

'I'm trying, dear, I'm trying!' gasped Israd.

But the ravenous sarcosuchus loomed ever closer behind them, gaining ground with every forceful thrust of its mighty tail.

'Arrrgh! A river monster!' yelled Torp.

Despite Israd's desperate efforts, the vicious brute was now only five meters behind, its mouth gaping open menacingly - *ready to bite!*

Danny could see that they were no more than about 20 meters away from the river bank now. But he could also see how quickly the sarcosuchus was advancing on them. For every meter Israd swam, the deadly brute swam about three.

They were never going to make it!

Danny desperately began to think.

Surely there was some way out of this perilous situation? Something he could do to prevent the looming attack from the deadly beast which was now drawing ever closer to them by the second. He racked his brains for an answer.

Then he remembered the dragon's tooth.

Of course!

He quickly fumbled in his pocket, knowing that every second counted. In an instant his fingers clasped around the ivory incisor lying snugly between the folds of the soft fabric and he hastily drew his hand out again.

The Monster From The Deep

He then held up the dragon's tooth in front of him in order to make his wish.

'I wish that...'

SLAM!

Danny was stopped from completing his sentence by a colossal impact from behind. The sarcosuchus was now attacking Israd! Having now caught them up, it had launched itself headlong into the Stegosaurus's side, its vicious jaws trying to clamp hard onto her body.

Fortunately, a Stegosaurus's hide is very thick and blubbery like a walrus's, and the sarcosuchus's jaws couldn't get a proper grip. Its head thrashed wildly about, its teeth snapping and gnashing and chomping but its teeth couldn't penetrate even a centimeter into the hard skin and it immediately crashed back into the water again with a gigantic splash.

'Help!' yelled Israd in alarm, trying frantically to regain her balance from the impact. Her body rolled and bobbled from side to side in the water, her legs urgently paddling this way and that in order to keep herself upright.

'Try and keep calm, Israd!' cried Danny, gripping tightly onto the bony plate with his free hand so he wouldn't over-balance and fall into the water. 'I'm going to use the dragon's tooth to make a wish that the crocodile thing will disappear.'

'Well, dear - make sure you make it disappear a long way from here!'

'Arrrgh! A river monster!' yelled Torp.

Danny And The Dinosaurs

'Oh, I do wish you'd stop saying that!' said Israd as she hastily made for the river bank again.

Once more, Danny held up the dragon's tooth in front of him.

'I wish…'

SLAM, CRASH, WALLOP!

The sarcosuchus had flung itself again at Israd's body, only this time the force was much greater than before. Its teeth gnashed, chomped and snapped. It's fearsome jaws trying once again to pierce through Israd's thick skin. But again, it failed and crashed down once again into the water below with a terrific splosh.

'Arrrgh!' yelled Israd.

'Arrrgh!' yelled Danny.

'Arrrgh*!* A river monster!' yelled Torp.

The collision was so forceful and sudden that Danny's whole body was launched forwards into the air, the dragon's tooth he was holding shooting out of his hand like a bullet and flying high up towards the sky.

'Oh, no! The dragon's tooth!' cried Danny despairingly as he found him self soaring through the air. But then all thought of his precious possession was quickly forgotten as he desperately tried to make a grab for one of the other bony plates on Israd's back. His fingers tried to cling on but he was flying too fast and the plate slipped through his grasping fingers. He made a grab for another… then another… then another.

Oh, no! thought Danny in panic. *He couldn't get a hold of any of them! And he would soon be heading straight into the water with the* sarcosuchus *and certain doom!*

The Monster From The Deep

But then, just as he was about to fly right over Israd's head and into the icy river below, his right hand managed to get a grip around the very last plate on Israd's back. He swung his other arm quickly sideways and clamped his left hand onto it too. He gripped on tightly for all he was worth as his flying body was suddenly jolted to an abrupt stop. His belly and legs slammed hard into the side of Israd's body with a loud, bone-crunching thud.

'Ouch!' he cried in pain.

But he still clung onto the plate as firmly as he could. His feet, however, were now dangling dangerously into the river water and he frantically tried to heave himself upwards onto the safety of Israd's back.

Unfortunately, he was so winded by the impact that he didn't have the strength to haul himself up. He heaved and he heaved, but it was no good! He could only manage to lift himself about half a meter up Israd's side before his strength gave out.

His feet continued to dangle in the water hopelessly as he hung limply against the side of Israd's body.

He was now a sitting duck!

He felt like a worm on the end of a fisherman's rod. *The sarcosuchus was bound to notice his feet any second now and then it would rise from below the surface, open those enormous jaws and gobble him up in a flash!*

'Hang on, dear boy - hang on!' cried Israd. 'We've only got a short distance to go now before we reach the river bank. I can feel the river bed under my feet now.'

'Arrrgh! A river monster!' cried Torp.

89

Danny And The Dinosaurs

'Oh, do shut up, dear!'

Israd was right. Danny turned his head and saw the bank was now only a few feet away. Maybe he would be okay after all, he thought.

But just then, he heard a terrific splashing sound from behind him as a huge, cascading wave of water rose up from the surface of the river. He looked around to see the most terrifying sight he had ever seen!

The sarcosuchus had swum up from the depths of the river at a terrific speed and had launched itself right out of the water like a missile. It was now careering through the air towards him, a nightmarish vision of ravenous jaws, razor sharp teeth and twisting flesh!

Danny froze in terror, his muscles locked rigid in fright-filled panic. He closed his eyes and screwed them tightly shut to block out the sight of the fearsome apparition which was hurtling towards him at break-neck speed.

He dangled there, helplessly - waiting for the inevitable; the sound of snapping jaws, gnashing teeth and the feel of fiery breath upon his face as the hellish monster from the deep closed in upon him and gobbled him up in one go!

The sarcosuchus hurtled towards Danny, rolling and swiveling its body. Ten meters away… Seven meters away… Four meters away… It opened its mouth wider - ready to bite!

Two meters away!

One meter away!

Then…

THWACK!

The Dragon's Tooth

The noise was deafening. It was so loud Danny thought his eardrums would burst. He grimaced. *Was it the sound of the sarcosuchus gobbling him up?*

No, he didn't think so. He didn't feel any piercing teeth chomping at his bones and biting through him. In fact, he didn't feel any pain at all.

SPLASH!

What was that? Something huge plunging into the water. Strange... He decided to carefully open one eye to see what was going on, still fearful of what he would see when he did.

His eyelid slowly opened a little and he squinted at the scene around him. *Where was the sarcosuchus? He couldn't see it!* He opened his eye fully. There was no sign of the hideous beast! There was just a circle of foamy, rippling water a few meters away, which was obviously the location of where the big splash took place.

He suddenly caught movement through the corner of his eye and looked around to see what it was. And there, flying up into the sky to his right was a pterodactyl.

Was it Rodak?

'We're here at last, my dears!' cried Israd suddenly, breaking Danny's train of thought. 'We made it, we made it!'

Danny opened his other eye and looked around more carefully. They were now heading up the river bank and out of the water.

He couldn't believe it!

Relief flowed through his entire body and his heart skipped a dozen beats. He was so happy!

Israd staggered slowly up to the top of the river bank, her exhausted legs barely able to work properly. Torp followed closely behind.

When they reached the luscious, green grass beyond, Danny dropped to the ground and lay there on his back, panting with relief.

Israd sat down with a thud, her lungs breathing heavily after her incredible exertions. 'Oh, deary me!' she wheezed. 'What a journey that was! I thought that horrible monster was going to eat us all up!'

'Oh, that big dino-fish was no match for me!' cried Torp. 'I wasn't afraid of it - not one bit. I was waiting for just the right moment to give it a good biff on the nose and send it scuttling right back down to the bottom of the river with its tail between its legs.'

Danny couldn't believe what he was hearing. 'Now, hang on a minute...' he began, but then he caught

Israd's knowing smile. Her smile quickly broke out into a chuckle and Danny soon found himself joining in, laughing heartily until his sides began to ache.

Torp just stared at them, without the slightest hint of shame.

'What did I say?' he asked when the laughter had died down.

'Okay, if you were so keen to punch that giant monster on the nose' said Danny with a smile, 'why didn't you?'

'Well, I was just about to,' insisted Torp. 'I'd drawn my arm back like a coiled spring and my right hand was clenched like a fist of concrete. I'd taken aim and was just about to punch the great brute as it flew by when THWACK!'

'Yes, I heard that too!' said Israd. 'What on earth was it?'

'It was Rodak,' explained Torp. 'He'd swooped right down from the sky, raised his feet out in front of him and knocked that ugly monster sideways - right back into the river.'

'So that was what that big splash was!' said Danny.

'Yes. And you should have seen the look on the monster's face when Rodak hit him. It didn't know what was happening.'

Just then a soft whooshing noise came from the sky above their heads and they all looked up to see Rodak gliding down to the ground to join them.

He landed with a soft thud on the grass, closed his wings carefully, puffed out his chest importantly and then looked down his long beak at the three travelers.

'Oh, Rodak - I could kiss you!' gushed Israd.

'That will *not* be necessary, madam!' replied Rodak with a horrified expression.

'Well, thank you anyway for saving us from that ghastly river monster,' said Israd, gratefully.

'Yes, we would have been certain goners if it hadn't been for you,' agreed Danny. 'Thank you ever so much! It was lucky you was around.'

'There was no luck about it,' replied Rodak. 'I have been following your progress from high up in the sky ever since you first set out. Brintus asked me to keep an eye on you in case you ran into any kind of trouble.'

'Well, it's a jolly good job he did,' said Israd. 'Good old Brintus, he's a very wise and clever old dinosaur.'

'He certainly is,' agreed Danny.

'Yes, well never mind about that now,' replied Rodak. 'I haven't got all day to chat about how smart and wonderful Brintus is. Goodness me, I have a lot of very important things I need to be attending to. This is no time for idle chit chat.'

'Oh, don't be such a grumpy old sourpuss!' said Israd.

'Madam, we need to concentrate on the job in hand. Time is very much against us, you know. Professor Zoran could have his magic spell ready at any moment. Now, listen very carefully to what I have to tell you.'

Danny, Israd and Torp listened attentively.

'When you reach Professor Zoran's castle, it is vital that you find your way straight up to the roof top. Don't waste any time searching any of the rooms for Draco.'

'Why not?' asked Torp.'

'I was just coming to that,' replied Rodak. 'Now please don't interrupt!'

'Sorry.'

'As I was saying before I was so *rudely* interrupted: Don't waste your time searching the rooms of Evilstone Castle. Very early this morning I flew over the Great Forest and had a good look at it. And there, right on the roof top, was the great dragon, Draco. *That's* where he's being held prisoner.'

'Thanks for letting us know,' said Danny. 'That will save us a lot of time.'

'How was the poor dear?' asked Israd.

'He was in the most terrible state,' said Rodak. 'Strong, thick ropes bound his mighty wings and held his body firmly down. He couldn't move even an inch. And his face! What a sad picture of total misery and abject despair, it was.'

'Oh, deary me - that's horrible,' said Israd with a worried frown. 'Poor old Draco. I do hope we can rescue him.'

'Of course we can!' shouted Torp. 'We've come this far, nothing can stop us now!'

'I wouldn't be too confident yet, young Torp,' replied Rodak. 'There are still great dangers ahead for all of you. Remember, you are not on Dino Island now. There are no friendly dinosaurs in the Great Forest, and many great beasts roam within its confines who would not think twice about chomping you up into little pieces and gobbling you for their dinner.'

Danny And The Dinosaurs

'I'm not scared of them,' said Torp, brashly. 'One quick biff from my fist and they'd be flat out on the floor wondering what day it was.' He bounded about on the grass, pumping his fists into the air like a boxer.

'Hmmm…' replied Rodak with an unconvinced tone. 'And even if you manage to avoid all the beasts of the forest, you will still have to get past all of Professor Zoran's men, sneak into the castle and climb up to the roof without being detected. It certainly won't be easy.'

'My, you're certainly a ray of sunshine, aren't you, dear?' said Israd.

'I'm merely pointing out the difficulties in store, that's all. That way you are better prepared for what faces you.'

'Well, I'm glad you will be around to watch over us,' said Danny.

'Oh no, young human. That is out of the question! I may have the strongest and most sharp-sighted vision in the whole of Dino World, but even I cannot see through trees! Once you are in the Great Forest I won't be able to keep track of you from the air.'

'No, of course not.' said Danny, his heart sinking a little.

'Don't worry,' said Torp as he gave Danny a friendly slap on the shoulder. 'You've still got me to look after you!'

'Yes, but if only I hadn't lost the dragon's tooth,' said Danny. 'It flew out of my hand when the river monster knocked me off Israd's back.'

The Dragon's Tooth

'You mean this?' said Rodak as he raised one of his claws in the air and dropped something on to the ground. Its white surface glinted in the light from the early evening sun.

Danny looked at it in disbelief. 'It's the dragon's tooth!'

'Indeed it is. I caught it when it flew out of your hand,' replied Rodak. 'It's a good job I am a very fast and skilful flyer, otherwise it would have disappeared into the depths of the river and been lost forever. And then where would you be?'

'Oh, thank you so much!' said Danny as he bent down and picked it up. He carefully placed it back into his trouser pocket and looked gratefully at Rodak.

'Yes, well try and be more careful in future,' replied Rodak sternly. A dragon's tooth is a very precious and powerful thing.'

'I will!'

'Now then, I can't stay here chatting to you all day,' said the pterodactyl, curtly. 'I've kept my word to Brintus, but now I simply must be off. I've lots of vital business to take care of elsewhere.'

And with that, he opened his enormous wings and began to run along the grass. His spindly legs carried him quickly over the grass, letting the air lift him gently off the ground. In a few seconds he was airborne and soaring up into the blue tinted sky. He then swooped down to his right, straightened out and flew low past the three travelers.

Danny And The Dinosaurs

'Don't forget,' the dinosaur cried as he glided past their heads, 'head straight to the castle roof! That's where you'll find Draco!'

And with that he was gone.

The three travelers watched in silence as the pterodactyl flew high over the Great River, his mighty wings beating gently to a fro.

Soon he was just a small speck in the late afternoon sky, a pin prick of movement silhouetted against the cloudy canopy above. Gradually, he disappeared from view altogether.

'Is it true what he said about how difficult it will be to save Draco?' asked Danny.

'Oh, don't listen to old Rodak,' said Torp. 'He's nothing but a grumpy old sourpuss!'

'Don't speak rudely about your elders, dear,' said Israd, curtly. 'Rodak may be a little stern and grouchy at times but his heart is in the right place.'

'Mmmm, I suppose so,' replied Torp, unconvinced.

'Now, I'm going to have a nice sit little down while I rest my aching legs,' continued Israd, wearily. 'That river crossing has all but worn me out. If I walk another step, I think my legs will come loose and fall right out of their sockets!'

Israd made herself comfortable in the grass and sat there for about half an hour, quietly dozing. Finally, she woke up and declared herself ready to continue the journey. She slowly hauled herself up off the ground and gently stretched her rejuvenated body.

'Ooohhh, that's better.' She smiled contentedly. I feel ready for anything now!'

'Good, then let's get going!' cried Torp as he jumped to his feet. 'All this sitting around doing nothing will make my joints go rusty.'

Danny giggled and got to his feet. Soon they were on their way again - Danny riding on Israd's back and Torp scampering ahead.

The Great Forest was only a short distance away and as they approached it Danny marveled at how tall and thick the trees were. They seemed to stretch up to the sky forever. As they entered the gloomy interior Danny swallowed hard, wondering what dangers may be lurking inside.

Thick creepers and vines coated the floor and they had to pick their way carefully through the undergrowth to prevent themselves from tripping.

The sounds of strange and mysterious creatures screeched loudly through the air. Forest insects swarmed in the gentle breeze, biting at Danny's skin. He swatted them away and wiped his sweating brow. He felt bad for Israd having to carry him so far.

The walk was long and hard and they continued on for some time.

Then, suddenly, the forest animals went silent.

'Why has it gone so quiet?' asked Danny.

Israd froze, her eyes searching the shadows.

'Over there - T. rex !' shouted Torp. 'Run!'

An all too familiar roar split the air. *Oh no!* thought Danny. *Not again!*

Danny And The Dinosaurs

They took off as fast as they could. Tree branches whipped back as they hurtled through the forest. Torp ran on ahead, Israd galloping not far behind.

Danny ducked a low-hanging branch.

THUMP!

THUMP!

THUMP!

'RAAAR!'

Danny glanced back over his shoulder. A huge T. rex with gleaming green eyes sprinted after them, its nostrils flaring red in the low light. It bellowed again into the air.

'RAAAR!'

Israd drew level with Torp.

'W-where to, dear?!' she panted.

'Over there!' shouted Torp as he pointed to a rocky outcrop ahead. 'There's a cave we can hide in!'

Danny hunkered down low onto Israd's back like a jockey. They were going so fast he was afraid he was going to fall off. They quickly sped past Torp and headed towards the cave at a rapid pace, the ground below Danny a blur of motion.

Suddenly, a fallen tree trunk came into view in front of them. Israd just saw it in time and took a mighty leap over it.

'RAAAR!' roared the T-Rex.

THUMP!

THUMP!

THUMP!

The Dragon's Tooth

Danny looked behind him. Torp leapt into the air to clear the fallen trunk. Then, everything seemed to go into slow motion – Torp jumping, his left foot catching in the branches of the tree, and then Torp falling... down, down, down to the ground.

The T. rex was just behind him. It roared with all of its might.

'Stop!' shouted Danny to Israd.

The dinosaur skidded to a halt. Within seconds, Danny had scrambled from her back and landed on the soft forest floor. The T. rex continued to close in on Torp, who was tugging furiously at his trapped leg.

'I have to try and save him!' cried Danny to Israd. 'Quick, you run into the cave and hide in there.'

And with that, he rushed back in the direction of the oncoming T. rex...

Danny Saves
The Day

The T. rex leapt high into the air, its huge jaws snapping and its taloned hands scratching at the air.

The whole ground shook as it landed just feet away
from Torp.

'*Help!*' shouted the little dinosaur in terror. He
squirmed and wriggled, desperately trying to free his
trapped leg.

Danny sprinted over the soft ground, making sure
not to get his leg stuck like Torp had. The huge T. rex
snapped its jaws again, big ropes of drool hanging down
from its savage teeth. This close up, Danny could see
they were yellowed and jagged, with bits of uneaten
food still stuck in them.

Danny dived forward, grabbing hold of the branches
that had entangled Torp's leg. Quickly, he tried to pry
them apart. He gave them a strong tug and Torp's leg
came free with a 'pop.'

Danny And The Dinosaurs

Danny looked up to see the huge T. rex towering over them.

'Oh no!' shouted Torp. 'What are we going to do? We'll never outrun him now.'

The ferocious dinosaur let out a low, menacing growl and snarled at them. It's tongue flicked out between its jaws and licked its lips, greedily.

Danny could feel its foul smelling breath blowing over his face. He glanced at Torp who was shaking from head to toe beside him. Danny's mind whirled as he tried to think of a way out of this desperate situation.

He had to do something. But what?

The T. rex eyed them intensely. It slowly moved sideways, waiting for just the right moment to launch itself at them. It crept forward, its soulless eyes never leaving them for a second. Its nostrils snorted blasts of hot, rancid breath into the humid air.

Danny racked his brain for an idea. As he did so, both he and Torp inched backwards, away from the advancing T. rex.

There must be something he could do! Think! Any second now that T. rex is going to pounce. Think! Think!

Then, like lightning, an idea suddenly zapped into his head.

'I've got it!' he cried.

He sprung to his feet. At the very same moment that the ferocious T. rex launched itself forward to attack him, Danny leapt sideways and dived onto the ground.

The T. rex had missed him by inches!

Danny Saves The Day

Danny somersaulted forward a couple of times before rolling onto the soft ground and quickly clambering to his feet again.

The T. rex roared an angry bellow as it stood upright again. It didn't like missing its prey. It now glowered at Torp who was still sitting on the ground in petrified horror.

The T. rex moved towards him, its mouth widening over its hungry jaws. Saliva dripped from its teeth like treacle. The cold, reptilian eyes on the top of its head narrowed in vicious intent. Closer and closer it came, its massive feet crunching the branches underneath.

Closer... And closer...

'Here! Over here!' Danny suddenly shouted, waving his arms and jumping up and down on the spot.

The T. rex stopped in its tracks and turned its massive head away from Torp. It stood still and glared at Danny.

'Come and get me you big, stupid, dinosaur!' shouted Danny again.

'W-w-what are you doing?' stammered Torp.

Great plumes of hot, foul breath continued to billow from the T. rex 's nostrils. It looked at Torp and then at Danny, its cruel eyes flashing with savage ambition. Then the great beast looked at them both again, swiveling its monstrous head to look at Torp, and then back to Danny again.

It now seemed confused as to who it wanted to eat first.

It sniffed the air.

'Hey, ugly head! Yes, you! You great, big, smelly lump!' called Danny. 'Over here! Come and get me.' He ran forward towards the great dinosaur and stuck his tongue out at it.

Well, that certainly seemed to make the T. rex 's mind up!

It spun around and lurched towards Danny with a mighty roar from deep within its lungs.

'RAAAAAAR!'

Danny quickly ran away in a wide, looping circle and scurried around a big Wollemi tree, the T. rex running after him in hot pursuit.

'You silly, big smelly-pants!' shouted Danny.

The T. rex roared in anger.

Danny circled around the Wollemi tree again. The T. rex followed, nostrils flaring, jaws snapping, fect stomping.

But it just couldn't catch Danny. The T. rex was just too big and cumbersome to run quickly enough around the massive tree. Danny was small, quick and nimble and he easily avoided the giant, clumsy dinosaur.

He ran around the tree again.

And again.

And again.

And again!

The T. rex followed, desperately trying to catch him.

'RAAAAAAR!' it bellowed as it ran around the tree after him.

Danny Saves The Day

Each time Danny ran around, he hurled insults into the air. And the more he ran, the faster the great dinosaur tried to run in order to try and catch him.

And as it did so, Danny could see it getting dizzier and dizzier and dizzier! Soon it began to stagger a little, its legs becoming wobbly underneath its giant body.

His idea was working!

He continued to circle the tree, scampering quickly around its enormous girth with the T. rex in hot pursuit.

Around and around they went.

'Come on, you great bumbling lizard!' cried Danny. 'You're too slow!'

The T. rex shook with anger and frustration. It tried to run faster but as it did so it tottered abruptly to its right and went crashing head first into the tree trunk with a mighty thud.

The tree shook violently under the impact.

'RAAAAAAR!' the T. rex bellowed in pain and fury.

It tottered upright again, trying to regain its balance. Then it launched itself forward again after Danny.

But it was no good. Danny darted off again around the other side of the tree.

The dinosaur followed.

'Can't catch me, you big, stupid reptile!' shouted Danny. By now he was also feeling a little dizzy, too. But he knew that the far larger and taller dinosaur would be feeling it a lot more than him.

Danny continued to run around the mighty Wollemi tree, the T. rex following after him, bellowing, snorting and snarling. But with each completed circle of the tree it got dizzier and dizzier and dizzier.

Around and around and around they went…

It staggered.

It tottered.

It wobbled.

Finally, Danny ran right away from the giant tree and headed towards a large bush about twenty meters away. When he reached it he stopped and turned around, waiting for the T. rex to appear from around the other side of the tree. When it staggered into view he frantically waved his hands in the air and called out to it.

'Come and get me, you great stinky jaw head!'

'RAAAAAAR!'

The T. rex blundered towards him, trying to run in a straight line. But it couldn't. It's body wanted to go in a completely different direction to its legs! It swayed to its left, tottered forward and then wobbled to its right. Then its eyes crossed, its legs buckled and with a great, ground-shuddering thump, the T. rex plummeted to the floor.

CRAASHHH!!!

The ground shook beneath Danny's feet as if there were an earthquake. He was quivering with relief.

'Woo hoo, you did it!' yelled Torp.

Danny slumped down onto the ground, tired from all the running. He head was spinning a little, too. He knew they didn't have much time to escape before the T. rex recovered, but he needed a few moments to rest.

Danny Saves The Day

Torp scurried over to the T. rex, who lay in a heap on the ground, rubbing its head and panting heavily.

'Not so big and scary now, are you?' teased Torp, skipping around the dizzy dinosaur.

'Torp, don't!' warned Danny.

Torp hopped from foot to foot, sticking out his tongue at the T. rex. 'Stinky-breath, stinky-breath!'

'Torp!'

'Look at you now! Fooled by someone smaller than you. All the other T. rex are going to laugh at you,' he cat-called.

The T. rex suddenly let out a huge roar and then its hand suddenly snaked out and grabbed Torp by his waist!

It lifted the terrified dinosaur into the air towards its gaping mouth.

'Arrrgh!' squealed Torp, suddenly losing his bravado.

'Torp!' yelled Danny, leaping to his feet.

The T. rex's jaws opened wide and hovered over Torp's head. Danny's gaze searched the ground. He quickly grabbed a thick branch from the floor.

'Raaaaaaaar!'

Just as the T. rex's mouth was about to swoop down and gobble Torp up, Danny ran forward, leapt into the air and jammed the branch between its jaws, preventing them from closing.

The T. rex was so surprised its hand flew open and Torp fell to the ground with a bump.

'Ouch!'

Danny And The Dinosaurs

'That won't hold him for long,' said Danny as the T. rex struggled to remove the branch that had locked its jaw open.

'What are we going to do?' asked Torp as he clambered up from the ground.

'The dragon's tooth!' cried Danny, pulling it out of his pocket.

An almighty snap suddenly cracked through the air. The T. rex had broken the branch! It turned towards them and staggered unsteadily to its feet.

'Raaaaaaaar!'

Danny quickly placed the dragon's tooth next to his heart. 'I wish...I wish that the T. rex's teeth would all fall out!' he cried. Then he rubbed his hand against the dragon's tooth and waited for something magical to happen…

There was a pause, and then the tooth suddenly glowed brightly in Danny's hand; a deep, emerald green which fizzled and sparkled shimmers of vibrant, dancing light. Then, as suddenly as it had appeared, the light faded and disappeared.

A series of small pops suddenly broke the forest air. Danny gazed up at the huge T. rex. He watched in amazement as one by one its teeth started to pop right out of its mouth and fall onto the ground.

POP!

POP!

POP!

The T. rex stood there in stunned surprise, its eyes open wide in confusion. It gazed down in horror at its teeth on the ground. And as it did so, even more teeth uprooted themselves from its gums and popped out of its mouth.

POP!

POP!

POP!

Soon, every single one of the T. rex's teeth lay on the forest floor in a great big pile. The bemused dinosaur could only look down forlornly at its precious canines.

'Quick, let's get out of here,' said Danny.

He grabbed Torp's hand and ran in the direction of Israd who had been watching everything from the safety of the cave.

She walked out to greet them.

'Well done, dear!' she said to Danny excitedly. 'Well done! You were ever so brave to take on that horrible brute of a T. rex. And to get it to chase you around that tree so it would get all dizzy and fall over was very clever! Very clever indeed!'

'I was just about to suggest that very idea myself before Danny started to run around the tree.' said Torp.

'Oh, you big fibber!' replied Israd.

'I was!' insisted Torp. 'I could see that Danny was really scared and frightened and wondering what to do. But, of course, I was icy cool and not afraid at all. Then the idea came to me. Danny must have read my thoughts, because at that very moment he started to run towards the tree.'

'I'll give you ten out of ten for your imagination!' replied Israd tartly.

'Come on, guys - we need to get out of here,' said Danny as he clambered onto Israd's back.

Soon they were trotting through the forest once again, the forlorn bellows of the bewildered T. rex growing fainter and fainter behind them.

'That was a close shave,' said Torp.

'Too close,' said Danny. 'Too close for sure.'

A Battle Of Life And Death

The three travelers lapsed into silence as their journey continued, each lost in his own thoughts. Danny, riding atop Israd's back, trailed his fingers over the leaves hanging down from the vast trees around him. He was tired from their adventure with the T. rex, but at least they had gotten away safely.

He just hoped the T. rex wouldn't find them again. Or any other T. rex, for that matter. There were probably lots more of them lurking about in the vast forest. He'd had enough high speed chases for one day!

After some time, they reached a clump of thick, tall bushes covered in berries. They carefully pushed their way through and emerged onto a wide, open clearing.

The ground was muddy and littered with bulrushes. Danny glanced up at the orangey-blue sky overhead and wiped beads of sweat off his forehead. It sure was warm here.

As they made their way across the clearing, keeping close to the trees by the side,

the ground became muddier and muddier underneath the dinosaurs' feet. And the further across the clearing they got, the deeper and more gooey the mud became.

'This dreadful stuff is making my beautiful feet all dirty!' complained Israd with a frown.

'Keep going, we should be out of it soon,' said Torp a few meters in front.

They continued on, but the mud became thicker and thicker and deeper and deeper. Soon it became an effort to even raise one foot in front of the other. The mud was so thick it gripped tightly onto their feet, sucking them down like a vacuum cleaner.

'It feels like I'm walking in the sticky glue from a gumuia bush,' grumbled Israd.

Danny peered across at the trees to the side of them. Was it his imagination or were they getting taller?

'Uh oh!' said Torp, coming to a stop.

'What is it?' asked Danny.

Israd and Torp exchanged glances.

'I think I'm sinking,' said Torp, looking down at his feet.

'Me too,' observed Israd. 'My lovely feet are sinking fast into this mucky sludge.'

Danny looked down at the muddy ground beneath them and sure enough, Israd was submerged up to her knees in the stuff. He looked back at the trees on the far side of the clearing.

A Battle Of Life And Death

The trees weren't getting bigger...*they* were sinking!

'Hurry up!' said Torp. 'Let's get to the other side as quick as we can.'

They started to move faster across the clearing. But with every step they took, they sunk a little deeper into the gooey mud.

Deeper and deeper and deeper...

Danny looked at Torp. The little dinosaur was now almost up to his waist in swampy mud and had to work hard just to move the slightest inch.

'We must be in a bog!' cried Danny in alarm.

'Oh my goodness!' cried Israd. 'Whatever next!'

'I can't move my feet!' cried Torp suddenly. 'They're stuck fast!'

'Do not worry, dear,' said Israd. 'I'll just wade over to you and you can then climb onto my back.'

Israd moved forwards, but each step was more difficult than the last. The mud became thicker and deeper with every step and her feet sunk lower and lower into it.

Suddenly Israd stopped and groaned.

'What's the matter?' asked Danny.

'I'm stuck!' yelled Israd. 'My poor feet are trapped in the mud too!'

'Oh, no!'

'Help!' yelled Torp. 'I'm still sinking!'

And sure enough, as Danny watched in mounting alarm, Torp steadily sank deeper and deeper into the bog. Soon the dark, sticky sludge reached up to his arm pits.

Israd was also sinking further and further into the black sludge. Danny looked down and he could see it creeping further and further up her legs.

'We need to do something quickly!' called Danny.

'Help, help, help!' wailed Torp in fright. 'I'm about to be gobbled up by a horrible bog! He frantically wriggled and jerked his body as he tried to free his trapped feet.

'Keep calm, and keep still!' warned Danny. 'The more you move about the faster you'll sink.'

'We're doomed!' yelled Israd. 'Dooomed!'

'Don't worry, I have the dragon's tooth!' said Danny. 'I'll soon save you both.'

'Oh, that won't work, I'm afraid,' replied Israd forlornly. 'It will only help its owner if they're in danger. You are the owner, not me or Torp. Save yourself - we're gonners. We're both doomed, I tell you. Dooomed!'

Of course! Israd was right about the dragon's tooth. Danny remembered what Brintus had told him when he handed it to him. Brintus's words echoed through his mind:

'It will only protect you, Danny... it will only protect you...'

Well, there was nothing for it, then, thought Danny. *He'd have to save them himself!*

He glanced upwards and saw an overhanging branch. Standing on his tiptoes on top of Israd's back, he reached up and curled his fingers around the branch. With a grunt of effort, he pulled himself up and climbed onto the branch and into the safety of the tree.

'On no!' said Danny when he looked down.

A Battle Of Life And Death

Both Israd and Torp were sinking faster and faster into the mud. It was now almost all the way up to Israd's shoulders and the top of Torp's neck!

'Heeeelp!' cried the little dinosaur's head, which was the only part of him which was now visible.

Danny quickly pulled himself along the branch towards Torp, his legs wrapped around it to stop him toppling off. The branch began to bend downwards the further out he got. Danny hoped it was strong enough to hold his weight and prayed it wouldn't snap.

The bark was rough against his fingers and covered in small twigs which scratched and pricked his skin. But he ignored the pain and climbed on. Further and further out he went, the branch bending lower and lower towards the dank, dark abyss below.

'Hang on, Torp, I'm coming!' he yelled.

Soon he was about three-quarters of the way along the branch. He could see Torp's head directly below him. The mud was now right underneath the little dinosaur's chin, and he had tilted his head back so he could still breathe.

'Quick, pull your arm out of the mud and reach for my hand!' cried Danny.

The little dinosaur grimaced and tried to move his arm upwards. But the mud was as thick as treacle and gripped at his arm like a vice. He strained his muscles for all he was worth and tried to force his arm out of the mud.

Then, slowly it started to move. Just a little, but it gave Torp encouragement and he continued to force his arm towards the surface of the bog, grunting and groaning under the strain.

Then, a hand appeared out of the mud.

'That's it!' cried Danny. 'Keep going!' He lowered himself down from the tree, his left hand gripping tightly to the coarse bark, his legs still wrapped securely around the branch.

He outstretched his hand towards Torp's, but it was still too far away to reach.

'I can't reach your hand,' cried Danny. 'Push it higher!'

By now the mud had reached as high as Torp's jaw and the little dinosaur couldn't tilt his head any further back. Danny watched in alarm as the black, treacle-like substance began seeping into the dinosaur's mouth. Torp coughed and spluttered before spitting it out.

'Close your mouth and breathe through your nostrils,' urged Danny. 'Now quickly, raise your arm higher!'

Torp struggled against the thick mud and tried to force his hand further out. And little by little it started to rise. First his wrist could be seen, then part of his arm and then his elbow.

Danny stretched out his arm as far as he could. Torp's hand was now only inches away from his grasp.

So near, yet so far!

Danny strained every sinew and muscle in his arm to make it longer, desperately trying to reach Torp's hand. But it was no good, he still couldn't reach!

He looked at the branch he was holding onto and noticed there was a smaller branch attached to it that was lower down and nearer to the surface of the bog. *If he could hold onto that instead of the main branch, his body would be closer to Torp and he'd be able to reach the dinosaur's hand.*

The only problem was that the branch was a good deal thinner than the main one. Would it be strong enough to hold his weight? What would happen if it snapped?

Well, he knew the answer to that! But Danny didn't waste any time thinking about it. His friend was in great danger and there was no time to lose.

He quickly repositioned himself, held his legs even more tightly around the main branch, and then let go of it with his hand.

His upper body immediately dropped downwards, and as it did so Danny made a grab for the thinner one.

Got it!

His hand tightened around it like a vice, and he held on for all he was worth.

He then outstretched his other arm again, extending it out towards Torp. A wave of excitement and relief washed over him as he felt the dinosaur's fingers against his. Just a little more and he'd have a firm grip. Danny stretched his arm out even more, desperately trying to get a tight hold of Torp's hand.

And then it was gone!

Danny Uses The Dragon's Tooth

Danny was gripping thin air!

He looked on in shock as he saw Torp's arm slowly descending back into the bog. The mud was starting to pull the dinosaur's body down again!

He'd missed his chance. If only he'd tried using the thinner branch sooner!

There was a sudden gurgling sound and Danny's mouth widened in horror as he saw Torp's head disappearing completely below the surface of the bog. Little bubbles of air floated to the top and twinkled upon the black, sludgy surface like stars against the night sky.

Danny's mind raced. *What could he do?! There were only seconds left before it would be too late and Torp would be gone forever!*

'Oh, poor Torp!' wailed Israd sadly, a tear forming in her eye. 'And I'll be joining him too, soon!'

Danny And The Dinosaurs

By now the mud was up to her shoulders, and rising. 'Goodbye, Danny, dear,' she sobbed, 'it's been very nice knowing you.'

There was no time to waste! Without thinking of his own safety, Danny let go of the branch he was holding and let his upper body drop down even closer towards the surface of the bog. Danny felt a jarring pain in his hip joints as his legs, still gripping tightly to the main branch, suddenly halted his drop. He winced in discomfort as he hung there upside down, swaying uneasily from side to side.

When he had gathered himself, he looked down towards Torp and almost froze in horror. The only part of Torp now visible was his hand!

'No!' Danny cried as he watched the little dinosaur's fingers disappearing down into the blackness of the bog. He flung out an arm and made a grab for Torp's hand.

Just out of reach!

Then an idea came to him. He began to swing himself backwards and forwards, using his stomach muscles to move his upper body. He began to swing back and forth like the pendulum on a grandfather clock.

Once he was swinging enough, he waited until he was moving towards Torp again and then made another grab for the dinosaur's hand. This time he caught hold of the fingers sticking out of the bog, but Danny wasn't close enough to get a good grip. His heart sank as he felt the fingers slipping away through his hand.

Danny Uses The Dragon's Tooth

Damn!

Danny swung away again and then mustered all his strength to swing further towards Torp on the next stroke. He grunted as his stomach muscles strained under the effort and then twisted his upper body forwards as hard as he could.

This was surely his last chance to save Torp!

His body swung forwards again, faster this time. As Danny lurched through the air he made one last desperate grab for Torp's fingers. His arm extended outwards, his muscles and tendons stretching so much Danny felt like his arm was going to pop out of its socket.

As he swung forwards he saw Torp's fingers getting closer and closer. Then, just as they were about to disappear from view forever, Danny felt his hand clasping firmly around them and he held on as tightly as he could.

Got him!

Danny immediately began pulling the fingers up, and with his other hand he reached down below the surface of the bog and got a grip of Torp's arm. Danny pulled and pulled for all he was worth and slowly but surely the dinosaur began to rise to the surface.

Then, with a loud sucking pop! Torp's head suddenly appeared, completely covered in thick, gooey mud. The little dinosaur spluttered and coughed and took in huge lungfuls of air as he desperately gasped for breath.

He remained there for several moments while he recovered. But by now, Danny's legs were getting tired.

Danny And The Dinosaurs

'Hurry, Torp!' he shouted, 'Start climbing up my arm and body and get to the branch. I don't know how much longer I can hang on for.'

The little dinosaur did as he was told and started to clamber wearily up Danny's arm. The mud squelched and plopped as Torp's body slowly rose from the surface of the bog. Danny winced in pain as the dinosaur's claws pierced his clothing and scratched his skin as the dinosaur gradually climbed upwards.

Torp slowly but surely heaved himself up Danny's body and onto his shoulders, covering Danny's clothes in black, squelchy mud. The stink was unbearable!

'Hurry!' shouted Danny. 'My legs can't hold on much longer!'

With one last gasping effort, Torp reached out with his hands and hauled himself off Danny's shoulders and into the safety of the tree. As he did so, his left foot caught Danny full on the nose.

'Hey!'

'S-sorry,' panted Torp as he collapsed onto the tree branch, breathing heavily.

Despite the pain to his nose, Danny felt relief that the weight of the little dinosaur had now been taken off his legs. But he was still hanging upside down and had to get himself upright onto the tree again. He began swinging back and forth so he could grab onto the smaller branch. From there, he could then reach the main branch with his hands and get himself the right way up again.

Back and forth he swung, the air swooshing about his ears. Then, he reached out and made a grab for the small branch. *Got it!* He gripped it tightly and then carefully maneuvered himself into position so he could grab onto the main one.

In a few moments Danny was sitting safely next to Torp.

He sighed with relief. But his satisfaction didn't last for long.

'Goodbye, dear friends, goodbye!' wailed a dejected voice from below. 'I'm dooomed! Dooomed, I tell you!'

Danny looked down in alarm.

Israd!

The large dinosaur was now up to her neck in mud. Her sad, baleful eyes looked back at Danny with hopeless resignation.

There was no time to rest! He had to rescue her before it was too late.

'Quick, Torp - we have to save Israd!'

But the forlorn dinosaur shook her head.

'No, save yourselves. Go on without me. There's no way you can pull me free, I'm too big and heavy. Oh, I do wish I'd stuck to that diet...'

'We can't let Israd perish!' cried Torp. 'If only you could use your dragon's tooth. But it'll only work if *you're* in danger.'

'That's it!' shouted Danny.

'What?'

'If I jump into the bog, then I'll be in danger, too! Then I can make a wish to save us both.'

'Hey, that's very clever!' replied Torp. 'I was just going to suggest that idea myself.'

Danny And The Dinosaurs

Danny reached into his pocket, took out the dragon's tooth and gave it to Torp to hold. He then quickly took his shirt and trousers off and hung them on a nearby branch. Next, he took his sneakers and socks off and placed them in a large hollow he found in the wood.

He took back the dragon's tooth from Torp, and gripping it tightly in his hand, he edged along the branch he was sitting on so that he was directly overhead Israd.

The dinosaur was sinking fast. The mud was now up to her mouth and she was struggling for air.

Danny perched himself on the edge of the branch and prepared himself to jump in.

'Gosh, I hope this works,' he said nervously as he summoned up as much courage as he could.

'I'm dooomed! Dooooooomed!' wailed Israd from below. The mud then started to seep into her mouth and she had to close it quickly.

There wasn't a second to lose!

Danny took a deep breath, closed his eyes then tipped himself over the edge. A couple of seconds later, he fell into the mud with a mighty PLOP!

However, it was a lot thicker than he had thought and as he landed into the muddy gunk his right hand slammed hard onto its surface. Such was the strength of the impact that it knocked the dragon's tooth clean out of Danny's hand and the magical canine flew off into the air, landing in the mud nearby with a soft, squishy squelch.

Danny lay there in the bog, dazed, dizzy and cold. The mud was as chilly as ice! Luckily he had landed

Danny Uses The Dragon's Tooth

more or less upright, but he was already up to his knees in it. He could feel the syrupy sludge clawing and grabbing at him, sucking his body down and drawing him deeper and deeper into its swampy embrace.

He looked over at the dragon's tooth, lying half exposed on the surface just a meter or so away.

Now, if he could just walk a couple of paces he could pick it up...

Danny tried to move his legs but they were stuck fast. He leaned toward the tooth and outstretched his arm but it was tantalizingly just out of reach.

It was just a fingertip away! He tried to lean further forwards but the more he leaned, the more the mud sucked at his legs and pulled him under.

'Oh, no! I can't reach the dragon's tooth!' he yelled to Torp. 'It's just out of reach!'

'Hold on!' Torp replied. 'I can help!'

Danny watched as the little dinosaur climbed down the tree trunk and then along one of the lower branches that overhung the bog. The dinosaur then clambered along it towards Danny. The branch bowed down dangerously under his weight as he did so and Danny was scared that it would snap at any minute.

But it held firm, and soon Torp was perched precariously right above Danny's head. He carried on, climbing further and further along the branch and further out above the bog.

Suddenly a cracking sound was heard, like wood splintering.

'Stay still!' cried Danny, 'the branch is weakening!'

Danny And The Dinosaurs

Torp froze… The sound stopped.

Danny breathed a sigh of relief. 'That's enough, now. Don't go any further out or the branch will surely snap right off the tree.'

'I think I've gone as far as I need to, anyway,' replied Torp. 'The tooth is right underneath me now.' He quickly wrapped his long tail around the branch and lowered himself down over the bog. His long, thin fingers stretched out towards the dragon's tooth.

Closer, closer… nearly there… *That's it!* He grabbed a hold of it and pulled it out of the mud.

'Can you catch it if I throw it?' he asked Danny.

Danny nodded. He glanced worriedly at Israd, whose nose and eyes were the only thing left above the swamp.

Torp hurled the magic tooth towards Danny. Stretching to the highest height that he could, Danny reached up and made a grab for it. The tooth was splattered with mud and for a split second Danny thought it was going to slip right through his fingers and go winging away across the swampy bog. But he clasped his hand tightly around it as if his life depended upon it - which it did!

'Good catch!' cried Torp.

As Israd's head disappeared under the bog, Danny gripped tightly onto the dragon's tooth and held it next to his heart. As he did so, he felt himself suddenly sinking faster and faster into the blackness of the swamp. It had now reached up to his shoulders.

Danny Uses The Dragon's Tooth

'I wish this bog was only as deep as my knees' he cried. He then rubbed the dragon's tooth with his hand and waited for something magical to happen...

There was a pause, and then the tooth suddenly glowed brightly in Danny's hand - just like it had done the last time he made a wish. The same deep, emerald green which fizzled and sparkled shimmers of vibrant, dancing light. Then, as suddenly as it had appeared, the light faded and disappeared.

There were a few seconds of silence and then suddenly a strange gurgling sound issued up from below. Danny looked down and saw the mud starting to slowly sink down his body.

The wish was working!

It was as if a plug had been pulled out from the bottom of the bog and the dark, oozy mud was disappearing down a great big hole. Danny watched in relief as the mud fell below his shoulders... then below his waist.. And then finally it stopped at his knees.

He then felt something beneath his feet. Something hard and solid... *Yes... it was the floor of the bog!*

Danny looked across at Israd, anxious to know if she had survived her horrible ordeal. *Had he saved her in time?*

The poor dinosaur was lying on her side in the mud, motionless. 'Israd!' Danny yelled in alarm. He quickly waded through the thick goo, almost falling as he desperately scrambled towards the stricken dinosaur.

He arrived by her side and a sudden look of horror spread across his face.

Danny And The Dinosaurs

Israd's eyes were closed, with not a flicker of movement to be seen. Her head hung limply in the black mud, her tongue jutting out between her teeth and hanging lifelessly across her lower lip.

Danny felt her belly with his hand. It was as still as rock - she wasn't breathing!

'Oh, no!' yelled Danny in anguish. 'Israd! Please don't die!'

By now Torp had climbed down from the tree and had joined Danny by Israd's lifeless body.

'Were we too late?' Torp asked, his eyes wide with concern.

Danny gazed up at him forlornly, a tear forming in the corner of his eye. 'She's not breathing,' he replied. Danny turned back to Israd and wrapped his arms around her neck and sobbed. 'Please wake up!' he cried. 'You can't leave us!'

He buried his head in the thick folds of Israd's skin and cried. He had only known her for a short while, yet in that time he had grown to love the brave dinosaur who had risked her life on this perilous journey in order to save her friends.

He couldn't believe that this horrible thing could have happened, how his dear friend was now lying lifeless before him on the floor of a muddy bog in the middle of nowhere, so far away from the friends she'd been trying to help.

And now she'd paid for her bravery and kindness with her life.

It wasn't fair! She didn't deserve this!

Danny Uses The Dragon's Tooth

Danny began weeping uncontrollably. Large, diamond shaped tears cascaded down his face in a river of sadness and bitter regret. He cried and he cried, his shoulders shaking violently as he cried out his anguish.

'No, nooo!' he wailed. 'Israd! We need you!'

Danny held even tighter to Israd's neck, not wanting to let her go, not wanting to accept that his dear friend's life had been so cruelly taken from her. And as he wept, his shoulders and arms shook in despair. He slightly jerked Israd's neck back and forth underneath him as he wept.

And this led to a most miraculous occurrence. As the dinosaur's neck moved up and down, the mud which had become lodged in her airway and which was the thing that had prevented her from breathing, moved too. Only a little, but it was just enough to open up a little gap… *Just* enough to allow some air in to her lungs…

The dinosaur wheezed slightly as the air rushed through the little hole. And as it did so, it pushed even more mud out of the way, widening the hole even further. More air then rushed downwards, deep into Israd's chest and into her lungs.

The wheezing increased to a gasp, then a splutter, then a cough. Mouthfuls of sludgy goo suddenly shot out of the dinosaur's mouth in violent bursts.

Israd was alive!

Danny released his grip and shot backwards as the dinosaur began wheezing, gasping, spluttering and coughing. He landed on his butt in the mud and stared at the dinosaur in disbelief and overwhelming joy.

131

Danny And The Dinosaurs

'Israd!' he cried. 'You're okay!'

'Yippee!' yelled Torp and began dancing around the bog with his arms in the air. Mud began splashing everywhere, but he didn't care. Nor did Danny. Their friend was back and they were overcome with happiness.

'Oh, I do feel rather queer!' panted Israd in a weak voice. She gasped some more, breathing in huge lungfuls of welcoming air, her great chest heaving in and out.

'Oh, Israd, it's so great you've survived,' said Danny. 'We thought you were a goner.'

The dinosaur didn't reply. She was too busy catching her breath.

Torp continued to prance and skip about in joyful celebration. As he did so, he sang a little rhyme:

'Israd's okay!
Hip, hip, hip hurray!
We thought she was gone,
But now she lives on,
And the smelly old bog's sunk away!

'Our mission can continue quite soon,
To defeat Professor Zoran, the buffoon.
I'll whack his big belly,
And turn it to jelly,
And smack his nose so it looks like a prune!'

Danny giggled and looked at Israd who was now recovering her breath. She wasn't breathing so heavily now, and the gasps and wheezes had subsided somewhat.

Danny Uses The Dragon's Tooth

'I think you could do with a drink of water,' said Danny.

'Oh, yes, dear, that would be wonderful,' replied Israd in a low, rasping voice. 'My throat is so coated in that ghastly sludge that I feel like I've swallowed a dozen mud pies.'

'There's a stream over there, beyond the trees,' said Danny pointing. 'Do you feel ready to walk yet?'

'I'm not sure, dear,' replied Israd, 'but I'll give it a try.' Slowly, she clambered unsteadily to her feat. It was clear that she was still weak and shaky after her death-defying ordeal. But she bravely began making her way over the floor of the once deep and mighty bog, Danny and Torp walking by her side. And slowly but surely the three travelers sloshed and waded their way across.

When they reached the stream Israd lay down by the shallow bank and dipped her mouth into the refreshing water. She drank and drank, feeling the cool liquid caressing her throat and washing all the mud away.

Meanwhile, Danny and Torp made their way back across the bog and to the tree where Danny had left his clothes and shoes. They returned to find Israd looking much better and happier.

She greeted them with a friendly smile.

'This water tastes wonderful,' she said. 'I think it's the tastiest water I've ever drunk - do have some, dears.'

'We will,' replied Danny. 'But first we need to wash all this mud off ourselves.' And with that, he and Torp waded into the icy stream and began cleaning themselves.

Danny And The Dinosaurs

When they had done, Danny climbed out and dried himself with the large leaves of a nearby plant and put his clothes and sneakers back on.

He sat down beside Israd and laid his head against her side. 'Ah, that's better,' he said as he closed his eyes. 'I feel so tired after all that…'

He gazed up at the darkening sky and sighed.

The sun was quickly retreating behind the distant mountains beyond, the blackening sky revealing softly twinkling stars that glinted like diamonds as the night welcomed them into its world.

Torp came over and lay down next to Danny. He too was exhausted after the day's adventures.

'I suppose,' yawned Danny, 'we had better find somewhere to bed down for the night…'

But within a few seconds he had fallen fast asleep.

Professor Zoran's Castle

By the time Danny woke up again it was early next morning, the first rays of the sun gilding the ground gold and amber. He opened his eyes and gazed blearily around him.

'Ah, you're up, dear boy,' said Israd who was already on her feet. She was happily munching away on a large, green leaf.

'What time is it?' asked Danny as he sleepily scratched his head.

Israd looked at him quizzically.

'Oh, I forgot - you don't use clocks here,' continued Danny. 'Never mind.'

'What a beautiful morning it is,' continued Israd. 'I've had a nice bath in the stream and I've been having these delicious dinglegoozle leaves for my breakfast.

'Dinglegoozle leaves?!' said Danny.

'Yes. The leaves of the dinglegoozle plant are the most succulent and mouth-watering thing you can eat in Dino World. Dinglegoozle plants are quite rare, and only grow in certain places. We're very lucky to have found one.'

Although Danny was very hungry, he didn't much like the look of the huge leaf Israd was happily chewing on. Still, the rumbling in his tummy told him that he should at least eat something. *Maybe the dinglegoozle leaf wouldn't be so bad after all.*

He walked over to the bushy plant beside Israd and took hold of one of the huge, thick leaves and pulled it off its stalk. He sniffed it carefully. It had a slight smell of liquorice. *Promising,* Danny thought. He inspected it thoroughly, turning it over in his hands to make sure there were no creepy crawly things lurking anywhere underneath.

When he was satisfied that it was safe to eat he took a little nibble from the end. It was kind of crunchy as he bit into it and then a sweet liquorice taste was released which filled his entire mouth with its pleasurable flavor.

'Hey, this is quite nice!' said Danny as he took a bigger bite.

'I told you, didn't I?' Israd smiled. 'But wait until you reach the middle! The middle is the tastiest, yummiest and most scrummiest part.'

And she was right. When Danny's teeth took a chomp from the centre of the leaf the most delectable flavor he'd ever experienced tingled through his taste buds, fizzed over his tongue and sent wave after wave of pleasure ripples gushing and burbling around his entire mouth.

'Wow! This is incredible!' Danny exclaimed. 'I've never tasted anything like it. It sure beats the lettuce leaves my mom makes me eat back home!'

Soon, Danny had devoured several of the delectable leaves and was sitting on the grass rubbing his full stomach in satisfaction.

Suddenly he heard a loud snorting noise behind him. 'What was that?!' said.

'Oh, it's nothing to worry about, deary. It's only Torp snoring.'

Danny looked over his shoulder at the little dinosaur who was still curled up on the grass, several meters away.

'ZZZ-Zzzz-hngGGggh-Ppbhww-zZZzzzZZ...' Torp snored.

Danny giggled. 'He snores even louder than my Dad!'

'ZZZ-Zzzz-hngGGggh-Ppbhww-zZZzzzZZ...Watch out!... ZZZ-Zzzz-Zzzz... He's behind you!... ZZZ-Zzzz-Zzzz... Let me at him!... ZZZ-Zzzz-Zzzz... I'll biff him!... ZZZ-Zzzz-Zzzz...I'llbashhim!...ZZZ-Zzzz-Zzzz...I'llwhop him!... ZZZ-Zzzz–hngGGggh-Ppbhww-zZZzzzZZ...'

'I wonder what he's dreaming about,' laughed Danny.

'I have no idea, dear boy. But we can't let him dream the whole morning away, we must get going soon while the day is young. Why don't you wake him up?'

Danny sprung to his feet and trotted over to the slumbering dinosaur. 'Torp, wake up,' he said as he gently shook the dinosaurs arm.

Danny And The Dinosaurs

'ZZZ-Zzzz-hngGGggh-Ppbhww-zZZzzzZZ…Zzzz-Zzzz-hngGGggh-Ppbhww-zZZzzzZZ… Take that, you brute!…zZZzzzZZ…' continued the dinosaur, oblivious to Danny's attempts to wake him.

Danny tried again: 'Wake up, wake up!' he said - louder this time. He gave Torp a harder shake.

But it was no good. The little dinosaur just continued his dreamy sleep.

'ZZZ-Zzzz-hngGGggh-Ppbhww-zZZzzzZZ… That'll teach you!…zZZzzzZZ…'

'Torp, will you please wake up!' cried Danny, shaking him with both hands this time.

'ZZZ-Zzzz–hngGGggh-Ppbhww-zZZzzzZZ… I've defeated Professor Zoran… zZZzzzZZ…and his army of guards… zZZzzzZZ… Single handed!…zZZzzzZZ… I'm a hero!…zZZzzzZZ…'

Danny looked over at Israd in bemusement and shrugged his shoulders.

'Allow me, dear,' she said, trotting over. The big dinosaur carefully cleared her throat and then bent her head down so her mouth was close to Torp's right ear.

'*LOOK OUT - T. REX!!!*' she bellowed.

'ZZZ-Zzzz-Zzzz… *W…What?! Arrrgh! Help… Bwharrr! Heeelp!!!*' yelled the little dinosaur as he woke up with a start. He scrambled to his feet in a flash and started to dash across the grass like a bolt of lightning.

'Wait, where are you going?!' chortled Danny.

'T. rex, T. rex - run for your lives!' cried Torp as he hurtled across the grass as fast as his little legs could carry him.

It wasn't until he heard the shrieks of hysterical laughter behind him that he turned his head around.

He slowed to a trot as the sight of Danny and Israd met his eyes. They were doubled-up with mirth on the grass, tears of laughter in their eyes.

Torp stopped in his tracks and looked quickly around. 'W-where's the T. rex?' he asked in puzzlement. 'And why are you both laughing?'

'Come back and join us, dear boy,' chuckled Israd. 'There's some yummy dinglegoozle leaves for your breakfast.'

'Yes, that's all very well,' replied Torp as he began walking back to join them, 'but about this T. rex…'

'That was a rotten trick to play,' said Torp some time later, his belly full to bursting point with delicious dinglegoozle leaves.

'But you just wouldn't wake up,' insisted Danny.

'And the only thing I knew which would drag you out of your slumber was to shout something that would scare you,' added Israd.

'I-I wasn't scared!' insisted Torp. 'I'm not scared of anything!'

'Oh, really?' said Israd as she gave him a knowing smile.

'No, not at all.'

'Then why did you run off as though your butt was on fire?'

'I was, er… running towards where I thought the T. rex was. Yes, that's it! And I, er… was going to, er… give it a good bash on the nose…er… in order to rescue you both!'

'Ooohhh, you really are the biggest fibber in Dino World!' snorted Israd as she got to her feet. 'Now, we really must be getting off.'

Danny chuckled as he climbed onto her back. Torp scampered on up ahead, still insisting that he wasn't in the least bit scared of any T. rex.

The early morning mist coated the ground as they made their way through the forest. Danny doubted he'd *ever* been up this early before.

'Do we have far to go?' he asked after about an hour of walking.

Israd shook her great head. 'No, dear, it's not far at all now.'

Soon, they came to a thick thicket of trees up ahead.

'We're here, we're here!' cried Torp who was peering through the leaves. 'The castle is just on the other side of these trees!' He jumped up and down excitedly as he waited for his friends to join him.

'Sshhh! Quiet!' said Israd in a loud whisper. 'There will be guards patrolling around here, we don't want them to hear us.'

Danny suddenly felt wide awake. His heart began to beat faster and he felt his breathing becoming quicker.

This was it then - they'd finally arrived at the castle. Now was the moment of truth!

Professor Zoran's Castle

As he and Israd reached the thicket he ducked his head down to avoid the overhanging branches. The dinosaur entered the maze of trees and gently squeezed her large body between the narrow spaces between them. It took some time to get through as Israd had to weave this way and that in order to find the spaces which were large enough. Some of the trees were standing so close to one another that even Danny wouldn't have been able to fit between them.

Once on the other side, they found themselves standing on the perimeter of Professor Zoran's gigantic castle.

The building loomed up high above them, a hulking granite monster that nearly blotted out the entire sky. It was made from huge grey stones with windows barred by thick, iron bars.

Around the castle was a large moat, the water glistening and glinting in the morning sunshine.

'Wow! That's the biggest castle I've ever seen!' whispered Danny. 'How did he ever build such a colossal thing?'

'Many other men came here to build it for him,' replied Israd. 'They rode strange looking monsters with round things for feet.'

'Round things for feet?' replied Danny.

'Yes. And these strange monsters dug the ground up and carried the huge blocks of stone into the sky so the men could build this castle. At least, that's what Rodak told us.'

Danny And The Dinosaurs

'I don't think they were monsters,' said Danny.
'What else could they be?' said Torp.
'They were machines,' replied Danny.

Professor Zoran's Castle

'What's a machine?'

'I haven't got time to explain about them now. Ask Brintus about them when we get back. We need to find a way to get into that castle.'

Danny gazed high up to the roof. There, he could see guards standing on the parapets, long rifles by their sides. They were looking down, surveying the area below and keeping watch for any intruders.

'We have to find a way in without being spotted by those guards,' he said, pointing up to them.

'How are we going to do that?' said Torp.

Danny thought carefully. 'I know,' he said. 'We need a distraction. Something to focus their attention on while me and Torp sneak up to the castle.'

'Like what?'

Danny surveyed the surrounding area carefully, and then he saw them. A smile crossed his lips.

'Rocks!' he suddenly cried.

'Rocks, dear?' replied Israd.

'Yes, don't you see?'

'I'm afraid I don't. How are rocks going to distract the guards? They don't do anything. They just sit there on the ground, doing nothing.'

'Not if someone sends them flying into the moat!'

'Oh, I see! I can do that.'

'Cool!'

'And when the guards see and hear all the splashes coming from the water then they'll all gather together to try and see what all the commotion is about.'

'Exactly! And that's when me and Torp can sneak up to the moat from the opposite side while all the guards are looking in the opposite direction.'

'What a brilliant idea! You're such a clever and resourceful boy.'

Danny blushed.

'But how are we going to get into the castle once we reach it?' asked Torp.

'You see those bars on the windows?' replied Danny.

'Yes. But that's exactly what I mean. How are we going to get through them?'

'Not through them - *between* them!'

'Huh?'

'Look carefully at how big the spaces are *between* the bars.'

Torp looked carefully. 'Hey, you're right! Those bars are pretty far apart, aren't they. We're both quite small. I bet we could squeeze right between them.'

'I'm sure of it!' said Danny. They're obviously designed to keep big, dangerous dinosaurs out like T. rex. Professor Zoran didn't plan for small boys.'

'And small dinosaurs!' Torp grinned.

Their plan of attack conceived, Danny and Torp found a fallen tree log and carried it to the edge of the thicket. They then collected several large rocks which were scattered about the area and placed them side by side onto the top of the log.

'Now,' said Danny, 'when me and Torp get to the other side of the castle we'll give you a signal.'

'What sort of signal?' said Israd.

'I can do an impression of a sloonywarzangle bird,' suggested Torp.

'A sloonywarzangle bird?' said Danny. 'Goodness me, what a peculiar name!'

'It's a peculiar bird,' replied Israd. They live in the forest, here.'

'But what's peculiar about them?'

'They fly upside down.'

'Upside down?!'

'Oh, yes, dear. And very rude they are too. No manners at all. They are without question the rudest and most ill-mannered dino birds I have ever had the misfortune to meet.'

'Yes, well anyway,' said Danny, trying to get back to the matter at hand. 'When you hear the call, give these stones a whack with your long and powerful tail. Make sure you aim well, and send them hurtling over there into the moat. We've put them on this log so it'll be easier for you to hit them. Me and Torp will take it from there.'

'Right you are, dear boy,' said Israd. 'Right you are!'

'Well, goodbye,' said Danny as he gave her a hug. 'Thank you for everything.'

'It's been a pleasure, dear,' replied Israd with a beaming smile. 'When I've finished hitting the rocks into the water, I'll make my way back through the forest to the Great River.'

'I hope you make it back home safely said Danny.

'Oh, I'm sure I will. Now you take care, won't you dear?'

'Don't worry, I'll be fine.'

'Of course he'll be okay - he's with me! pointed out Torp.

'That's what I'm worried about!' replied Israd.

Danny giggled, but before Torp could protest, Danny took hold of his arm and ushered him away through the undergrowth. They crept away carefully, making sure to walk as quietly as they could. Eventually Israd faded out of sight, swallowed up by the green foliage.

To avoid detection, they kept to the edge of the trees which bordered the entire castle. And slowly but surely they made their way around; climbing over rotting logs, clambering through bracken and forcing their way through thick, rope-like vines.

But eventually they arrived on the opposite side of the castle and hid themselves carefully behind a large tree.

They peeped out from behind it and were amazed by the sight which met their eyes. There, lying behind the rear of the great castle, were rows and rows of iron cages, all lined up side by side in neat rows upon the ground. There must have been over a hundred of them, covering the area of at least thirty football pitches. They stretched off into the distance as far as the eye could see.

They were the biggest cages Danny had ever seen. They were absolutely enormous. Each one was as tall and as wide as a building!

'Professor Zoran's zoo!' said Danny in awe, 'Look at all those cages - they're absolutely gigantic!'

'They give me the creeps,' replied Torp with a shudder.

'Don't worry, they won't be having any dinosaurs in them,' said Danny, 'not if we have anything to do with it.'

He turned his attention to the castle and looked carefully for a way in.

'Look!' he said, there's a drawbridge.'

'What's a drawbridge?

'Er, well it's a kind of bridge that lowers down over the moat so you can get in. That's it, over there.' Torp followed Danny's pointing finger.

'Do you see it?' asked Danny. 'That big wooden thing?'

'Yes I see it. But it's closed.'

'Yes, I know. But, do you see? There's a window just above that section of the drawbridge which is connected to the castle. Once we've swum over to the other side, we can climb up the drawbridge and reach the window.'

'Yes, I see,' replied Torp, nodding his head.

'Okay, time to give the call, Torp.'

The little dinosaur cleared his throat and put his open hands to his mouth. He then raised his head to the sky and squawked a long, high pitch cry.

'*Ewwwwock-ca-ca-ca-ca!Ewwwwock-ca-ca-ca-ca!*'

They then closely watched the guards on the parapets, above. They were relieved to see that they paid no attention. They remained stock-still, not moving an inch. To them it was just another of the many dinosaur calls which emanated from the forest each and every day.

Danny And The Dinosaurs

Danny and Torp then patiently waited to see what happened next. Danny held his breath and crossed his fingers that they would do what he hoped for and all dash to the opposite side of the castle when the rocks started hitting the water.

They waited… and waited… and waited.

'There's nothing happening,' whispered Torp. 'They're not moving!'

Danny began to get worried. What if something had gone wrong? What if Israd had been seen by some guard patrolling the forest? What if she had been captured before she could hit the rocks into the water?!

Then, suddenly he spotted movement at the top of the castle. A guard in the far corner suddenly dashed to his left and disappeared from view. Then a guard to his right turned his head around and scurried out of sight. Then another guard disappeared. Then another… and another! His plan was working! In a matter of seconds the rest of the guards had all disappeared from view as well.

There was not a single guard on their side of the castle!

'Good old Israd!' whispered Torp. 'I knew she wouldn't let us down!'

'Now's our chance!' urged Danny. 'C'mon!'

He pulled Torp out from behind the tree and they both made a dash for the moat. They ran as fast as their legs could carry them across the short, stubbly grass and then dived head first into the icy water which surrounded the great castle.

Professor Zoran's Castle

It was absolutely freezing, but they both ignored the cold and started to swim furiously towards the castle as fast as they could. Danny's wet clothes clung onto his skin, making it awkward for him to move through the water, its cutting chill biting into his hands with every stroke.

Torp found it a lot easier. His smooth, scaly skin allowed him to carve through the water quite easily and he was the first to arrive underneath the cover of the closed drawbridge. He bobbed up and down in the water underneath, waiting for Danny.

When Danny arrived to join him he needed a few moments to catch his breath. He had never swum as fast in his life!

'Okay', he panted, 'now we climb up this drawbridge to reach the window. Torp glanced up at the big wooden drawbridge above them. It was constructed with long horizontal tree trunks held together with rope. There were large wooden blocks sticking out at regular intervals which were there to support the framework and stop the drawbridge from falling apart. These blocks provided a convenient ledge for any would-be climber to use.

But to get to the drawbridge they first had to climb up the stone exterior of the castle for several meters.

'I'll go first,' said Danny as he reached up. His fingers found a deep crevice that allowed his fingers to get a good grip of the stone and then he pulled himself up carefully.

He then swung his right leg sideways and searched for something to grip onto with his foot. Fortunately, the stones at the foot of the castle were not particularly smooth. They were rough and jagged and Danny soon found a nice craggy bit that held his foot firm. He then lifted up his left leg and found another foothold.

He then continued the process and slowly but surely ascended up the stone exterior of the castle. He then climbed onto the wooden drawbridge with Torp close behind him.

They then began steadily climbing up the drawbridge, using the wooden blocks as ledges to grip onto with their feet and hands.

Soon, Danny found himself right next to the barred window of the castle. He inched himself towards it as closely as he could, but it was still too far away to just climb onto. He would have to make a leap from the drawbridge and then grab onto one of the metal bars of the window.

He took a deep breath and then launched himself forwards, kicking hard against the wooden drawbridge with all his might. He sailed through the air for several feet and then made a grab for the bar and held on as tightly as he could. His lower body slammed against the castle wall with a thump and his feet dangled precariously in the air.

But he hung on grimly and then swung his right leg upwards and brought his foot down onto the window ledge. The rubber sole of his sneaker gripped hard onto the wood and then with a swift movement Danny swung his other leg up and found himself sitting safely on the window ledge, about thirty meters above the moat below.

Phew, made it!

He sat there for a few moments to rest and catch his breath. He then put his face right up against the window pane and peered inside the room to see if anybody was lurking about inside.

But it was very dark. All Danny could see were vague and ghostly shapes in the gloom of the interior. *Furniture,* he thought.

He listened… Nothing. The room was as silent as a grave.

Satisfied it was empty, Danny reached into his pocket and took out the dragon's tooth. He placed the sharper end close to the window pane and then with a sudden stabbing motion he jabbed it hard at the glass. The window pane immediately shattered, sending broken shards of glass crashing to the floor inside. Danny hoped that the noise hadn't alerted any of the guards on the roof.

He put the dragon's tooth back safely in his pocket and then sat quietly for a few seconds, listening carefully for any cries of alarm from up above. But all was silent. The only sounds to be heard were the distant screeches of some pteranodons soaring high in the morning sky above them and the bad-tempered squawks of a group of feathered mononykus who were squabbling over some food in the nearby trees.

Danny sighed with relief. *So far, so good!*

Next, he began to pull out the large fragments of glass that were still stuck in the window frame. After each piece had been removed, he lowered his hand through the window frame as far as possible and carefully dropped the glass so it would make as little sound as possible when it hit the floor.

When he'd finished, Danny then squeezed himself between the thick metal bars and perched himself on the other side of the wooden window ledge.

He peered into the darkened room beyond and listened again… Silence.

A few seconds later and he was standing in the room, beckoning Torp to join him.

The Iron
Time Machine

'This room is very dark,' whispered Torp as he jumped down off the window ledge, 'I can hardly see a thing.' His wet feet squelched on the floor as he walked, leaving a watery trail of footprints behind him on the stone surface.

'Well, it's only a small window and the sun is on the other side of the castle,' replied Danny as he gazed around in the gloom. 'There's not much light getting in.'

As their eyes began adjusting to the darkness, more strange shapes began revealing themselves from the inky shadows. Big shapes, long shapes, rectangle shapes, small shapes, square shapes…

Danny blinked, trying to focus his eyes and identify what they were. He walked blindly around, searching for the door. His knee suddenly banged into something hard.

'OW!' he cried in pain.

'Sshhh!' whispered Torp.

'Sorry,' replied Danny as he rubbed his knee.

'Where's the door?'

'I don't know, but it must be here somewhere.'

They continued wandering around the room for several minutes, searching for the way out. Gradually the shapes started to get clearer and clearer and Danny realized that he was walking between rows of glass display cases. What was in the cases he had no idea, it was still too dark to see.

Then, as Danny was losing hope of ever finding a door in this strange room, he saw a sliver of light on the floor in the far distance. *Gosh, how big was this room?!*

He decided to walk towards it, hoping it was what he thought it was. As he got closer he broke out into a relieved smile. *He was right, it was the door!* The light was from the room beyond, creeping underneath the gap between the door and the floor.

'Hey, Torp!' whispered Danny excitedly, 'I've found the door!'

He leaned his hand on the wall while he waited for Torp to join him. And as he did so, his fingers felt something jutting out from the surface. Something thin and pointy… *A light switch? He* tried flicking the pointy thing down with his thumb. There was a click, and then the room was immediately bathed in brilliant, dazzling light.

Danny had to close his eyes from the glare at first. His pupils had adjusted themselves for the gloom, of course, so it took several moments of squinting before he felt comfortable enough to keep them properly open and gaze around him.

What he saw when he did so took his breath away...

The room was absolutely enormous. The white ceiling loomed high above him in the distance like a gigantic cloud hovering overhead and the walls on either side were so far apart you could fit 2 school buses end to end between them and still have room for a couple of cars.

And filling this ginormous room were the rows of glass display cases that Danny had previously been able to only dimly see in the shadowy darkness. Row upon row stretched out before him in neat and symmetrical order; too many to count. And each individual row must have contained dozens upon dozens upon dozens of individual glass cases; some as small as footballs, others the size of televisions and some as huge as cars.

And now that Danny could actually see what each of these mysterious cases contained, his mouth gaped and he let out a gasp of shock.

For, in each and every one of the neatly arranged cases was... a dinosaur! Not alive, mind you - but stuffed. Stuffed in the same way that a taxidermist stuffs a dead lion or a polar bear so they can be displayed in museums.

Danny gazed in wonder at the cages. They contained dinosaurs of all shapes and sizes. There were iguanodons and spinosauri and protoceratops and micro raptors and troodontids - all easily recognizable from Danny's dinosaur text books. But there were countless dinosaurs he had never seen before in his life, all stretching out before him in this enormous, cavernous room.

This must be Professor Zoran's private collection of stuffed dinosaurs, thought Danny.

He was still gawking at the cases as Torp joined him by the door, a look of absolute horror on his face.

'What's the matter?' asked Danny.

'L-look at them!' cried Torp, pointing at the glass cases.

'Sshhh!'

'It's terrible - terrible!' continued Torp more quietly.

'What is?'

'Can't you see them!'

'The dinosaurs?'

'Of course!'

'Yes, amazing isn't it?'

'Amazing? *Amazing?!*'

'Yeah. We have stuffed animals back home in museums. I've been to see them on school trips. But we have nothing like this! I bet a museum would pay millions and gazillions of dollars to get their hands on just one of these stuffed dinosaurs…'

Danny's words trailed off as he saw the look of fear and sadness on Torp's face… and then he realized.

Each and every creature in these glass cages was a dinosaur… just like Torp! No wonder his friend was horrified. Imagine if they were stuffed human beings instead of dinosaurs - how would he feel?

Danny felt incredibly guilty and shameful that he could be so insensitive and unfeeling.

The Iron Time Machine

'Oh, I'm so sorry, Torp,' he said, putting his arm on the little dinosaur's shoulder. 'I wasn't thinking. Forgive me.'

'It's okay,' replied Torp, still eyeing the cases uneasily.

'C'mon,' said Danny, 'let's get out of this awful room.' He placed his hand on the door knob and turned it. There was a gentle click and Danny slowly pushed the door ajar and peered through the gap to look for any guards. Satisfied the coast was clear, he opened the door and walked through.

The room he found himself in was a lot smaller than the previous one, although the ceiling was just as high. It was completely empty except for a very strange looking metallic object that sat right in the very middle of the room.

Danny walked towards the mysterious thing, trying to figure out what on earth it was. It was very tall, about the height of two grown men and it seemed to be made of iron. It was oval in shape and looked rather like a deep see diving bell that divers used to take them down to the bottom of very deep oceans. Except this one looked old, very old, like an antique.

And all around the outside of this strange object were thick rubber tubes, criss-crossing over its metal surface like jumbled spaghetti. There were several holes drilled into the side of it and the ends of these tubes disappeared right into them like snakes diving into a burrow.

But perhaps the most interesting thing about the object was what was located right at the very front of it... a neatly fitted glass hatchway.

Danny And The Dinosaurs

Danny approached it cautiously and peered through the glass which must have been at least twenty centimeters thick. The inside resembled a cockpit, with a large leather seat secured to the floor in the middle. Located just to the side of the seat was a long lever and on the curved wall of the interior of the machine were all manner of metal wheels and small levers - just like the ones inside the driver's cab of an old steam train.

There were also several instrument panels on each side of the seat, consisting of rows and rows of valves, gauges, meters, switches, buttons and dials; all constructed from gleaming brass and which were fixed securely into an iron plate secured to the wall. And underneath each instrument was a little description which detailed its function, etched into the metal plate in neat gold lettering.

Danny read some of them. They said:

Light-speed Accelerator Thrusters, Antigravity Clutch Transformer, Plasma Radiation Gauge, Time Warp Brake Synchronizers, Hyperdrive Transmission Booster, Fourth Dimensional Space Loop Compressor, Force Field Suspension Dampners, Positronic Wormhole Mapping Frombulator, Time-stream Wurglewomp Paddlers, Neutronium Heat Shield SprongboozleWimperers.

Danny stood there in bemusement and scratched his head. *What did they all mean? And what on earth was this bizarre, unearthly contraption?* Although it looked as if it were made recently, it looked very old fashioned - positively antique. It looked like something made before the First World War.

The Iron Time Machine

'C'mon, Danny!' whispered Torp, standing by the door, 'we need to get going.'

'Yes, I'm coming,' said Danny. But just as he was about to turn around and walk away something inside the interior of the machine caught his eye. Danny stopped and looked more closely.

His gaze fell upon two wooden rectangular boxes which were fastened onto the wall behind the seat, one above the other. In each of the small boxes were several little windows and in each one of them was a white card on which was printed a date, time and year. The time was given in hours, minutes and seconds.

Danny watched and as he did so the numbers corresponding to the seconds in the little windows changed. They seemed to flip from one number to another as the time ticked by: *14, 15, 16, 17...*

Then the minute display changed, too. In the top rectangular box it changed from 45 to 46 and in the one below from 26 to 27.

Danny noticed that there was a little sign above each of these boxes. Above the top box it said: *Destination Time*. And the time displayed on this box read: 12.33 and 52 seconds. The month and year read: July 16th, *360,432,568 B.C.*

The second box had a sign above it which read: *Departure Time*. And the time displayed on this box read: 15.33 and 34 seconds. The month and year read: February 23rd, *1912 AD*.

Danny gasped as he finally realized what he was looking at.

Danny And The Dinosaurs

'Of course!' he exclaimed in a loud whisper.

Torp looked at him quizzically.

Danny stepped back a few paces and gazed at the iron contraption in awe and wonder.

'So *that* is how Professor Zoran has gotten here to Dino World,' said Danny excitedly as he pointed at it.

'What do you mean?' said Torp.

'This,' replied Danny, *'is a time machine!'*

In Search Of
The Dragon

'What's a time machine?' asked Torp.

'Well, it's, er, a machine which allows you to travel into the past or the future.'

Torp looked at him blankly.

'Let's say we both jumped into this machine now,' continued Danny as he tried to explain. 'We could travel in it to… say… tomorrow afternoon. Understand?'

'Not really. Why do we need to go into this machine thing to get to tomorrow afternoon? Tomorrow afternoon will come around anyway.'

'Yes, but that would take time, wouldn't it? This machine allows you to get to tomorrow afternoon, *today!*'

'Today?'

'Yes!'

'But if it's still today, how could we be in tomorrow?

Danny sighed.

Danny And The Dinosaurs

'Look, this machine allows you to travel to tomorrow *instantly*. You don't have to wait or anything. You just press a few levers and buttons and things and hey presto - you are in tomorrow.'

'And Professor Zoran used this to get here to Dino World?'

'Exactly! According to the instrument panel he left his own time at half past three in the afternoon of the 23rd of February, 1912.'

Danny gave the time machine a last, lingering look before heading to the door. As he walked, Danny's mind was teeming with thoughts and questions. It was pretty clear that Professor Zoran didn't come from Danny's time, but all the way from 1912.

Wow, that was two years before the start of the First World War! he thought. *No wonder the time machine looked really old-fashioned.*

But another thought struck him: *How did the professor get all the machinery here to build his castle? It would be far too big to get into his time machine. There would be diggers and cranes and mixing machines and things like that.*

And what about all his guards? There was only one seat in the time machine. How did they get here?

It was certainly a mystery, but Danny had to put all these thoughts to one side as he opened the door slightly and cautiously peered through the gap.

He found himself looking out into a long corridor. Slabs of smooth stone made up the floor, and softly burning torch lights hung at regular intervals from the walls, illuminating the scene with an orangey glow.

'C'mon!' whispered Danny. 'The coast is clear.'

They both quietly entered the corridor and started to tip-toe down it, listening carefully for any sounds of approaching danger.

'How do we get to the roof?' whispered Torp.

Danny thought for a few moments before saying: 'Well, there must be some stairs leading up to the upper floors of the castle. We just need to find them and keep going up until we get to the roof.'

They continued on, down the long corridor which after a time began to bend round to the left. The whole castle was eerily silent. Soon the corridor began to straighten out again, allowing Danny to see a large oak door standing ahead of them across the whole width of the passageway.

'I wonder what's behind that door,' he said as they approached it. Once there, he quietly turned the iron handle and heaved the heavy door open. It creaked complainingly on its hinges as he did so. Danny peeped though the gap and saw a large entrance hall spread out before him.

Danny gazed around.

To his left was a huge oak doorway, which was obviously the main entrance to the castle. In front of him was an enormous grand staircase which stood at the far end of the room, a thick red carpet covering nearly the entire length of each step.

Built into one of the walls to his right was an iron fireplace in which a pile of burning wood was roaring and crackling fiercely, the hot embers glowing like boiling suns.

Danny And The Dinosaurs

An enormous crystal chandelier hung down from the ceiling, towering above the room like a hovering spaceship, and in the middle of the floor stood a huge oak table. Fierce looking lions were carved into the legs, snarling, roaring and growling. And all around the walls of the cavernous room hung huge oil paintings of who Danny could only assume was Professor Zoran.

So this is what he looked like, thought Danny.

The man in the paintings had a long, curly black moustache and a short and neatly trimmed beard which came up to a point just below the middle of his lower lip. The lips themselves were thin and mean-looking, like a miser's.

His hair was wild and straggly, as if he'd been dragged through a hedge backwards and his long nose stuck out from his face like a giant carrot. His piercing brown eyes had a shifty look about them and seemed to be far too close together. They stared menacingly out from the canvas, giving Danny the creeps.

Each of the paintings showed the man in a different pose - standing by a statue, by a river, next to a horse, in a laboratory. There was even one of him standing next to the iron time machine. But in every one of the pictures the man had the same arrogant and evil-looking expression oozing out of every single pore of his face. There was definitely something strange and eerily malevolent about him.

What a horrible looking man, thought Danny.

His clothes looked terribly old-fashioned as well - but then they would if he came from the year 1912, he reasoned. On the man's head was perched a very tall top hat which was jet black in color and in some of the paintings he was wearing a long, dark cape which reached all the way down to his shoes.

'Let's get up those stairs before somebody comes!' whispered Torp, jolting Danny out of his thoughts. Danny nodded and they both crept out from the doorway and scuttled across the stone floor of the vast hallway and began to climb the great staircase.

They climbed and they climbed - higher and higher and higher. The staircase seemed to go on forever! Eventually they reached the top and found themselves on the second floor. Two corridors lay on either side of the stairs, stretching off into the far distance.

'Which way?' asked Torp, glancing left and right.

'We keep climbing,' replied Danny, pointing at another flight of stairs to their left. They were spiral, and wound slowly upwards.

'Goodness knows where those corridors lead to, but our best bet is to keep going up.'

They began to climb the second stairway but had gone no further than a dozen steps when the sound of men's' voices above them suddenly filled the air. Danny jerked back, almost sending Torp flying back down the stairs. He grabbed Torp's arm just in time and pulled him back to safety.

'Someone's coming down the stairs!' whispered Danny in alarm. 'It must be some of the guards!'

'What do we do?'

'Quick, this way!' replied Danny as he grabbed Torp's arm again. He pulled the little dinosaur down the stairs and when they reached the second floor landing again they quickly scampered down one of the corridors.

Glancing frantically ahead for somewhere to hide, Danny spotted a doorway to his left. He made a grab for the door handle and turned it.

Please open! Please open! he thought as he turned the handle and pushed.

But the door wouldn't budge. It was locked tight!

No!

The voices were getting closer and closer. Any second now and the men would be on the second floor landing - right in front of Danny and Torp!

Danny looked around anxiously and spotted another door opposite. He darted across to it with Torp close behind, his tail twitching in mild panic. Danny tried the door handle and this time the door swung open welcomingly as he pushed.

Danny breathed a mighty sigh of relief and the two dashed inside. He shut the door quickly behind them and then placed his ear to it and listened.

They had made it just in time! Danny could hear the voices of the guards and the clicking sounds of their feet on the stone floor of the corridor as they approached. From the sounds, he could tell there were two of them and they were getting closer and closer.

Please walk past! Please walk past! wished Danny.

Louder and louder grew the voices until they were right outside the door Danny and Torp were hiding behind.

The voices in the corridor suddenly stopped.

'Did you hear something?' asked one of the guards.

Danny held his breath.

His heart was beating so hard his rib cage was rattling. *What if they got caught? Everything would be lost!*

And then...

'No, it must just have been the wind,' said the other guard. 'This castle is full of noises. It gives me the creeps.'

'I know what you mean,' said the other guard. 'I'll be glad when I get some leave so I can go back home.'

'Yeah, me too.'

And then the footsteps continued down the corridor, softer and softer as they receded into the distance.

Danny let out a shaky breath as he heard the two guards walking away.

'They've gone!' He grinned at Torp who was looking at him anxiously.

Relief instantly washed itself over the small dinosaur's face.

'Right, let's go!' said Danny, peering out of the now half open door. 'The coast is clear.'

They made their way back down the corridor and began climbing the stairs once again. There were no more voices this time and their journey was undisturbed. The winding staircase went up and up and up and Danny's legs began to ache a little. Torp, too, was finding it a bit of a struggle. More so, in fact, than Danny.

They reached the third floor and then kept climbing - up and up and up, past the fourth floor... then the fifth... past the sixth...

Danny And The Dinosaurs

When they reached the seventh floor landing Torp slumped down onto the stone floor and sat there, panting heavily while he rubbed his aching legs.

'My legs aren't cut out for this stair climbing business,' he gasped. 'I'm not used to stairs and my legs are only little.'

'But we must keep moving,' Danny urged, even though his calves were throbbing quite badly. 'The guards could reappear any minute. We need to get to the roof as quickly as possible.'

'How many more of these stair case things have we got to climb? They're like mountains.'

Danny shrugged. 'I don't know. But we must be pretty high up by now - there can't be many more left to climb.'

After a few moments Torp struggled to his feet, grumbling under his breath about mountainous stair cases that went on forever.

Danny smiled as the dinosaur stood up.

'That's the spirit!' He grinned. 'We must be strong. Anything worthwhile requires effort. That's what my dad always says.' He then stopped in thought, remembering that his dad wouldn't even be born for another three-hundred and sixty million years. 'I mean, it's what my dad *will* say.' he corrected himself.

Gee, this time-travel business sure makes things confusing!

And so the two brave adventurers ventured on... up to the eighth floor... then the ninth and tenth floors.. Then the eleventh floor...

In Search Of The Dragon

Finally, when they reached the landing of the twelfth floor they found themselves in front of a large wooden door. A brass handle decorated the front, shaped in the head of a roaring lion.

There were no corridors left or right this time, neither were there any other rooms. There was nothing whatsoever apart from the door and an oblong window which was set into a small recess in the wall to the left of where Danny and Torp were now standing.

'I need to rest again,' said Torp as he collapsed onto the floor in a heap. 'I couldn't climb another one of those pesky stairs!'

'Well, it's a good job there aren't any more, then!' Danny grinned as he sat down beside him. 'We'll take a couple of minutes to rest, then we must get going again.'

After a few minutes, Danny stood up and walked over to the little window and peered out through the glass.

Wow, they were really high up!

Far below him the Great Forest stretched out like a green blanket, the tops of the trees rippling and swaying in the playful winds.

He could also see the Great River in the far distance, its surface twinkling and glinting as it reflected the light from the golden sun.

Then Danny glanced up and over to the right and he saw it - the roof of the castle! Part of it was jutting out from the towers below. But it was definitely the roof, he was sure of it because he could see the battlements. He'd learned about them at school.

Danny And The Dinosaurs

Battlements, his teacher had taught him, were comprised of a low wall about chest height in which rectangular gaps occurred at regular intervals to allow men to fire arrows at their enemies below. Danny even remembered what the gaps in the wall were called - crenels.

Danny looked carefully to see if he could detect any guards standing at the crenels, but there were non there. Well, not on the part of the roof that he could see, anyway. And he knew very well that if there were any guards skulking about it wouldn't be arrows they'd be firing, but guns!

The roof was probably about twenty meters higher than he was and Danny guessed that the wooden door nearby would lead right up to it.

But there was only one way to find out!

He dashed over to the door, took hold of the handle and turned it. Thankfully, it clicked open easily under his grasp and when Danny walked through he found himself in a short, gloomy passage way. At the other end, a few meters in front, was another large wooden door.

'C'mon!' he said, turning to Torp who was still sitting down on the floor outside, 'the roof is this way.'

Torp climbed to his feet and followed him inside.

Danny opened the second door and walked out to find himself standing in a small, brightly lit room. Candles shone enthusiastically from holders fixed onto the stone walls. The room itself was completely empty, but to the right a thin spiral stairway with iron handrails led upwards, flanked by a wall with several windows.

In Search Of The Dragon

'Oh, no - not more stairs!' complained Torp as he stepped out into the room.

'They can't go up very far,' replied Danny, 'the roof is quite near.'

'How do you know?'

'I saw it out of the window on the landing.'

'Okay, but you better be right. I think my legs are just about ready to fall off my hips at any minute!'

'We'll be up these stairs in no time, you'll see,' said Danny as they began to climb.

But no sooner had they taken their first step upon the staircase when there was a loud cash and the wooden door to the side of them suddenly burst open!

Danny and Torp shot their heads around in startled surprise. They looked in horror at the sight that met their eyes.

There, in the doorway, stood a mustached man in a top hat and long, black cape. He was flanked by several burly guards on either side.

'Intruders - get them!' snarled Professor Zoran, pointing menacingly at Danny and Torp.

Danny And The Dinosaurs

Professor Zoran Outlines His Plans

Before Danny and Torp could move an inch, several guards charged forward and grabbed them.

'Get off me!' shouted Danny as a pair of brawny hands clasped themselves around his shoulders and marched him roughly towards Professor Zoran.

Two other guards got hold of Torp and dragged him forward, too.

The two friends were then placed in front of the smirking Professor Zoran who stood there looking at them, his black moustache twitching and his beady little eyes sparkling with gleeful menace.

'Well, well, well - and what do we have here?' he snarled, his mouth contorting into a thin-lipped sneer.

Danny glowered at him, but said nothing.

'We have a small boy dressed in some very strange looking clothes and a little baby dinosaur,' continued the professor, eyeing them curiously.

Danny And The Dinosaurs

'I'm not a baby!' cried Torp.

'Well, you're certainly a trespasser! shouted the professor. 'This is my home you've been sneaking around in!'

He looked Danny up and down carefully with his small, beady eyes. 'By the way you are dressed I can see that you don't come from the year 1912, like me. What year have you time traveled from, little boy?'

'2014,' said Danny.

'Really?' the professor replied, looking rather impressed. 'I've never been further into the future than 1955.' He then bent down and pressed his face right up against Danny's, his cold, heartless eyes glaring with icy wickedness.

'And *what* are you doing here?'

'I'm not telling you!'

'Oh, I think you will.'

'I will *not*. I'm not scared of you!'

The professor snorted scornfully and stood up. 'I think I may have a way to persuade you to be more cooperative.'

'No you haven't. I'm not going to tell you anything!'

'Oh, yes, you will. Because if you don't, I'm going to shoot your little dinosaur friend!'

Danny gasped. 'You wouldn't dare!'

The Professor cackled manically before drawing a large pistol from a holster around his waist.

'You know, dinosaur shooting has become a rather passionate hobby of mine,' he said, looking at the gun admiringly. 'You may have come across my nice

174

collection of stuffed dinosaurs during your trespassing around my castle. Well, I'm proud to say that I personally shot every single one of those dinosaurs myself.'

He then pointed the gun at Torp and carefully cocked the trigger.

'Now, little boy - this is your last chance! Tell me what you are doing here in my castle or your little lizardy friend here is going to be blasted into a thousand tiny pieces!'

Danny looked at Torp, whose knees were trembling in fear, his face a mask of absolute terror.

'I'm going to count to three,' continued Professor Zoran coldly, 'and if you don't tell me what I want to know then I'm going to pull the trigger.'

He closed one of his beady little eyes, peered down the long barrel of his pistol and took aim at Torp.

'... One...' he said, slowly.

'... Two...' he continued, his finger tensing on the trigger.

'... Three!'

'*STOP!* Okay, okay, I'll tell you!' Danny blurted out. 'Just don't hurt Torp!'

The professor relaxed his finger and lowered his gun towards the ground. 'I knew you would soon come around to my way of thinking.' He grinned arrogantly. 'Now little boy - *why* are you here?'

'To rescue Draco,' mumbled Danny.

'Speak up, boy, I can't hear you!'

'To rescue Draco,' said Danny, more loudly.

'Draco? Who's Draco? Oh, you mean that ugly old dragon I've got imprisoned on the roof?'

'Yes.'

'And why do you want to rescue him? Is it to stop me from collecting his tears and building my magic bridge so that I can transport the dinosaurs to my nice, new zoo?'

'Of course! You have no right to imprison them in cages.'

'Why ever not?'

'Because they have a right to their freedom. They have done nothing wrong.'

'Oh, who cares about that?' The professor snorted. 'Have you any idea how much lovely money I'm going to make out of them?'

'You creep!'

The professor cackled manically and twisted one end of his thin moustache between his fingers.

'I don't think you appreciate the sheer genius of my plans, little boy,' he continued. 'Very soon, I am going to be the owner of the most popular zoo in the entire history of the world. Not an *ordinary* zoo, mind you, filled with boring animals like penguins, tigers and bears. Oh, no! But a zoo populated by real, live dinosaurs!'

He cackled again.

'Just imagine how many people will be willing to pay to travel back in time to visit a *dinosaur* zoo! Thousands, millions, gazillions! And they'll all be paying *me*! I'm going to be rich beyond my wildest dreams! Do you hear! Richer than all the kings and queens in the whole wide world put together!'

Professor Zoran Outlines His Plans

He rubbed his hands together and cackled for a third time.

'But your time machine only has room for one person,' pointed out Danny. 'How can you transport anyone here?'

'Oh, you silly little boy!' laughed the professor. 'Do you really think I've only got *one* time machine? How do you think I got all my guards here and the machinery to build my castle and zoo?'

'I don't know...'

'The time machine you saw while you were so *rudely* sneaking around my castle is my *personal* time transporter. There is another, far bigger one hidden in the grounds of the castle - as big as an airplane!'

Danny goggled in surprise.

'You see, little boy - I have thought of everything. I am a genius! The greatest genius that ever lived! My time machines are the greatest scientific inventions in history. While every other scientist was saying that time travel was impossible, my greater, far superior intelligence told me they were completely wrong. So secretly worked for years in my private laboratory, building, experimenting, testing, tweaking. Until one day I discovered it - the secret to traveling through time! I then built the world's very first time machine.'

'Well, you should use it for good - not for doing bad things to dinosaurs,' said Danny.

'Oh, who wants to be a goody-goody? Being bad is much more fun - especially if it can make me mind-bogglingly rich!'

Danny And The Dinosaurs

'You're a really horrid man!'

'And soon to be a very wealthy, horrid man!' Professor Zoran replied with a snigger. 'Now - there is one very important thing I need to know, little boy. How did *you* travel back in time to get here?'

'I'm not really sure,' said Danny. 'I was in my uncle's attic and I was cleaning the dinosaur's egg he'd given me, which really wasn't a dinosaur's egg after all but a dragon's. And then it suddenly grew really big and there was a large hole in the side of it and I looked inside and then I fell in. Then I found myself in a forest and I was chased by a T rex and then...'

'What on earth are you prattling on about?!' cried the professor in confusion.

'I fell into a hole, which had appeared in a magical dragon's egg after it grew,' said Danny. 'Then I fell out again and found myself transported back in time.'

'What a load of nonsense!' interrupted the professor. 'Everyone knows that dragon's eggs are not magical objects. Your story is bogus!'

'It's the truth!' cried Danny indignantly.

'Oh, I've no time to stand here and listen to the imaginative ramblings of a silly little boy! I'll get to the bottom of how you got here later.'

He glanced up towards the ceiling. 'Now - it's time to collect the very last few tears from that wretched dragon on the roof.'

Danny gasped. 'Do you mean...'

'Yes!' interrupted the professor, catching on to what Danny was going to say. '*Today* is the day that I finally

178

Professor Zoran Outlines His Plans

gather enough tears to create my bridge building spell! I'll have you know that as well as being a brilliantly clever scientific genius I'm also a master in the art of advanced magic. I studied under all the greats, you know - Wibblewobbler The Wand Caster, Fizzyburp The Sorcerer - even the Great Warnycrump The Conjurer!'

He then paused and looked from side to side at his guards. 'Right - there's no more time to waste! Up to the roof we go! Bring these two trespassers along, too. They can watch as I collect the last few tears from that wretched dragon!'

And with that the evil professor marched towards the stairway and began to skip up the stairs, two at a time.

'Oh, I'm so excited!' he shouted as he climbed. 'My dastardly plan will soon be completed and then I will be as rich and as wealthy as can be!'

The guards followed behind, pushing the forlorn figures of Danny and Torp up the long staircase.

What now? thought Danny as he climbed the steps, sad and dejected. He imagined all his poor dinosaur friends trapped behind the cold, iron bars of Professor Zoran's cages, their freedom gone forever.

No longer would they be able to roam freely whenever and wherever they pleased across the great plains and forests of Dino Island, but instead, they would be prisoners trapped in a zoo. Mere pawns in Professor Zoran's greedy quest for money and power.

Everything seemed lost.

Their plan had failed!

Or had it…?

Escape Bid

When they reached the top of the staircase Danny and Torp were pushed through a large wooden door and out onto the flat, stone roof of the castle.

Professor Zoran was already standing there, a mischievous look spread across his face. He gestured to a huge dragon which was lying on the floor, tethered to iron rings by long, heavy ropes.

'Look at how even the mighty dragon cannot defy me!' He laughed 'I'm too smart! Too clever! Too brainy! Nobody can out-wit me!'

He began cackling yet again, which was a peculiar habit Danny had noticed almost all villainous creeps possessed. He'd seen it on various television programs. Perhaps it was something they had to learn at Villain School, or something. Danny didn't know, but it sure was an annoying habit.

He gazed across at poor Draco. The dragon looked a very sorry sight, indeed. Bound tightly to the floor by the numerous strong ropes, it was hard to see how it could even move an inch. Danny couldn't even imagine how uncomfortable the dragon must be feeling after not being able to move properly for months on end, to not be able to stretch and loosen his muscles.

How cruel and heartless to keep a creature like this!

Escape Bid

The dragon's mighty wings were pressed down tightly against its body and were all crumpled and twisted by the strong ropes which bound him down. And upon its face was such an expression of sadness and despair that Danny's heart felt as if it were going to break. He felt so sorry for the poor creature, lying helplessly on the floor, at the complete mercy of the evil Professor Zoran.

As Danny looked on with sympathy, the dragon gazed mournfully ahead into the far distance, as if its mind were in a better place.

Professor Zoran ordered his guards to tie Danny and Torp's waists together with strong rope. Danny winced as the rope tightened uncomfortably around his skin.

'We don't want you running away, now, do we?' Professor Zoran chuckled. 'So don't even think about it. You won't get very far tied together like that.'

He looked across at one of his guards. 'Hand me that poker!' he barked. He then glanced back at Danny and smirked. 'Now we come to the really good bit!'

The guard did as he was told and walked over to a small metal stove standing at one corner of the roof. He opened the door carefully and Danny could see the twisting red and yellow flames of the roaring fire as the wood inside burned fiercely.

The guard took out a long iron poker which glowed brightly with intense heat, closed the oven door and then walked over to Professor Zoran and handed it too him.

'Now - fetch the buckets and go and place them underneath the dragon's eyes,' the professor ordered two other guards. They scuttled off to obey their order.

183

Danny And The Dinosaurs

Danny then watched in horror as the professor calmly walked towards the rear end of the dragon, an evil smile spreading across his lips.

'Now to make the dragon cry,' he sniggered as he waved the red hot poker about in the air. 'I always enjoy this bit!'

'No! Don't!' shouted Danny.

But Professor Zoran ignored him. 'Making dragon's cry is so much fun!' he yelled, waving the poker about even more.

'You brute!' shouted Danny.

'One more jab with this and the last few tears that I need will fall!' the professor cried triumphantly. He started to dance a little jig, swinging the poker high into the air and twirling around like a drunken ballerina.

'Poor Draco! There must be something we can do!' whispered Torp in Danny's ear. 'Wish the dragon free with the dragon's tooth.'

Danny shook his head. 'I can't. It only works if I'm in danger, remember?'

'Oh, yeah.'

Suddenly there was a drastic change in the dragon's expression, from one of deep sorrow to one of keen and enthusiastic interest - as if it had just heard something very, very important...

As the villainous professor continued to dance and jig around upon the rooftop, Danny suddenly heard a very strange and peculiar voice speaking to him. Now, I say it was a very strange and peculiar voice because it *wasn't* a voice from somewhere on the roof. Oh, no...

Escape Bid

It was a voice coming from right inside Danny's very own head!

And the voice was no ordinary voice. In fact, it was like no other voice Danny had ever heard before. It had a magical and almost bewitching ring to it as the words flowed one after the other in a deep, rhythmic tone. They were spoken in a soft and deliberate manner, as if each word had been carefully thought out before being spoken.

DO NOT BE ALARMED, MY FRIEND, began the very strange and peculiar voice. THIS IS DRACO THE DRAGON SPEAKING. I AM USING MY MAGIC MIND POWER TO COMMUNICATE WITH YOU SO PROFESSOR ZORAN AND HIS GUARDS CANNOT HEAR ME. IF YOU CAN HEAR MY WORDS, PLEASE NOD YOUR HEAD.

Danny nodded his head.

GOOD. NOW, I COULDN'T HELP OVER-HEARING JUST NOW THAT YOU HAVE A DRAGON'S TOOTH. IF THIS IS CORRECT, PLEASE NOD YOUR HEAD.

Danny nodded again.

Draco's eyes lit up in excitement. EXCELLENT! I DO BELIEVE THAT THE TOOTH YOU HAVE IN YOUR POSSESSION IS MINE. IT WAS SHOT OUT BY PROFESSOR ZORAN WHEN HE CAPTURED ME.

A DRAGON GETS HIS MAGICAL POWER FROM ONE SPECIAL TOOTH IN HIS MOUTH. WHEN MY MAGICAL TOOTH WAS SHOT OUT, I LOST MOST OF MY MAGIC. I ONLY HAVE ENOUGH LEFT FOR MIND MAGIC. I CAN'T EVEN BREATHE OUT FIRE

ANYMORE. THAT IS WHY THE EVIL PROFESSOR WAS ABLE TO CAPTURE ME.

NOW, IF YOU WOULD BE SO KIND AND BOLD AS TO PLACE THE TOOTH BACK IN MY MOUTH I WOULD BE EXCEEDINGLY GRATEFUL AS IT WOULD RESTORE MY MAGICAL POWERS AND I WOULD BE ABLE TO ESCAPE FROM THIS TERRIBLE CASTLE.

WOULD YOU BE WILLING TO DO THIS KIND DEED AND HELP ME?

Danny nodded eagerly.

THAT IS SO VERY GOOD OF YOU. NOW, MY FRIEND, YOU MUST BE VERY QUICK OR THE GUARDS WILL STOP YOU BEFORE YOU'VE HAD THE CHANCE TO PLACE THE TOOTH IN MY MOUTH. THAT WOULD BE DREADFUL - ABSOLUTELY DREADFUL. WE CERTAINLY DON'T WANT THAT TO HAPPEN, NOW DO WE?

Danny shook his head slightly.

IS THE TOOTH IN ONE OF YOUR POCKETS?

Danny nodded.

VERY GOOD. NOW, MY DEAR FRIEND, HAVE THE TOOTH READY IN YOUR HAND BEFORE YOU TAKE IT OUT. HOLD IT POINTY SIDE UP SO YOU CAN PLACE IT IN MY MOUTH AS QUICKLY AS POSSIBLE.

I WILL BLINK MY EYES THREE TIMES. THIS WILL BE THE SIGNAL FOR YOU TO RUN FORWARD. I WILL THEN OPEN MY MOUTH NICE AND WIDE FOR YOU. YOU WILL SEE A HOLE BETWEEN MY TEETH ON THE RIGHT HAND SIDE OF MY MOUTH. THAT

IS WHERE YOU SHOULD PLACE THE TOOTH. STICK IT IN NICE AND HARD.

DO YOU UNDERSTAND?

Danny nodded again.

SPLENDID, SPLENDID! ALRIGHT - WHEN YOU HAVE THE TOOTH READY IN YOUR HAND JUST NOD YOUR HEAD AND THEN WAIT FOR MY SIGNAL.

Danny gripped the tooth in his pocket and carefully maneuvered it with his fingers so the pointy side was facing upwards as the dragon had asked. When it was ready, he nudged Torp and whispered quietly to him.

'Listen carefully - I don't have time to explain, but Draco has talked to me and told me to run forward and put the dragon's tooth in his mouth.'

'Did he speak to you in your head?'

'Yes, but how did you know?'

'Dragon's are magical - everyone knows that. Mind Talking is one of their oldest tricks.'

'Oh, okay. But listen - our waists are tied together so we need to run forward at the same time.'

'But how do I know when to run?'

'Draco is going to blink three times. That is the signal that he's going to open his mouth so I can put the tooth in. After the third blink, I'll shout "run." Okay?'

'Yes, understood,' said Torp. He looked at the dragon's eyes and readied himself for the dash forward, his muscles tensed and his legs slightly bent so he could spring forward as soon as Danny had issued the signal.

Just at that moment Professor Zoran stopped dancing his jig and walked menacingly towards Draco. 'And now it's time to play Burn The Dragon.' He smirked, twiddling one end of his black moustache with the ends of his fingers. 'It's my most favorite game you know! I love to see all those lovely tears dropping down into my buckets.'

He thrust the red hot poker out in front of him and aimed it at a spot on Draco's green and scaly skin.

'Time to cry, dragon. Time to cry, ha, ha, ha!'

Danny took a deep breath and nodded his head at Draco. There was a pause and then the dragon blinked. Once...Twice... Three times!

'Run!' shouted Danny and he leapt forward. At the very same time Torp launched himself toward the dragon as fast as he could, careful to run at exactly the same speed as Danny so they wouldn't stumble and fall over.

The guards standing behind them were taken by complete surprise and Danny and Torp were away and running before they had a chance to stop them.

As Danny rushed towards Draco, the dragon opened his mouth as wide as he could, straining against the thick ropes tied around it. Fortunately, they had not been fastened as tightly as the others and he was able to force his mouth open wide enough for Danny to get his hand in.

Professor Zoran froze in surprise, the red hot poker just inches away from Draco's skin.

'Hey, what are they up to?! Stop them! Stop them!' he shrieked as he saw Danny and Torp hurtling towards the dragon. The guards did as they were told and quickly gave chase, their legs a blur of whirling movement.

Escape Bid

Within seconds Danny and Torp had reached Draco. Danny held out his right hand and plunged his head into the dragon's open mouth. He desperately began looking for the hole in the gum, but it was just too dark to see properly.

Quickly, he began feeling around the mouth with his free hand. At first he felt nothing but rows and rows of gigantic teeth, pointy and long like giant icicles of ivory.

Where is it, where is it?! Danny thought as his hand fumbled around for the hole. He knew he only had seconds left to find it before the guards would be upon him.

And then suddenly he felt something - a wide gap between two of the teeth near the front of Draco's mouth. Danny's hand reached down and felt the gum and there it was! A gaping hole.

As quick as a flash he positioned the tooth above the hole with his hand and then jammed it down as hard as he could.

PLOP!

It was in!

Just in time, too, for Danny suddenly felt two large hands on his shoulders and he and Torp were quickly dragged away from the dragon by the burly guards.

Professor Zoran scuttled over to them, his face contorted in anger.

'Trying to rescue the dragon, were you?' he cried, waving the hot poker at them. 'Well, you failed! You didn't really think you'd have time to untie all those ropes before my guards got to you, did you?'

He glared at them, his eyes blazing and his moustache twitching. 'How dare you try to ruin my plans!'

'How dare you imprison Draco!' said Danny.

'He's done nothing to you!' added Torp.

'Now listen to me you pair of wretched creatures,' said Professor Zoran, 'I've had just about enough of your pesky meddling into my affairs. I think you need to be taught a jolly good lesson... Yes, that's a great idea! When I've done with that stupid dragon over there I'm going to think up a nice punishment for you both. The more painful and horrible, the better! Ha, ha! Now, what could it be...'

He turned to one of the guards.

'Rigsby - What do you suggest?'

The guard thought for a moment. 'Erm.... Erm...'

'C'mon man, I haven't got all day!'

'Er, well what about making them go to bed early?'

'No, no, no! You fool! That isn't nearly as wicked and dastardly enough! The professor turned to another guard. 'Fletcher - what do you suggest?'

'How about not giving them any dinner?'

'No! No! No! You nincompoop! I want evil! I want nasty! I want the most hideously, unpleasant and beastly punishment imaginable. Rodgers - what have you to say?'

'Can I go to the toilet?'

'Arrrgh!!!! screamed the professor in frustration.

'Well, it's been ages since I last went,' the guard insisted, 'I've been patrolling around this cold and draughty castle all morning without even a break.'

Escape Bid

'I'm surrounded by idiots and dimwits!' yelled Professor Zoran, throwing his hands into the air and gazing up to the heavens.

'I suppose *I'll* have to think of something. Now, let me see…'

But as the Professor stood there and thought about what utterly cruel and gruesome punishment he could give to Danny and Torp, something strange was happening behind him.

He was thinking so hard, in fact, that he didn't hear the faint sound of dragon's breath upon the ropes, burning them gently free with carefully aimed puffs of wispy red and yellow fire.

But Danny, Torp and the guards did. They were all standing in front of the professor, their mouths gaping in surprise at what was happening behind him.

The tooth restored in his mouth, Draco the dragon's magical powers had returned!

And now he was carefully and precisely burning his ropey binds free!

'Er… P-P-Professor…' stammered a guard, his face a mask of horror.

'Not now, Simpkins - I'm thinking!'

'No, I really think you ought to know…'

'Be quiet!'

'But Professor…'

'Will you shut up!'

'But the dragon is…'

'Aha! I have it!' interrupted the professor with a smirk. He twiddled his moustache, which he always liked doing when he had thought of something deliciously evil and wicked to do. He bent down and looked Danny and Torp in the eyes.

'Your punishment will be this: I will take you out into the Great Forest and tie you both to a tree. I will then leave you there overnight at the complete mercy of the T rex and velociraptors and all the other vicious dinosaurs that roam around amidst the mighty trees and bushes. If you survive the night - which I very much doubt, ha, ha! - then I will bring you back here to my castle. And then - well - I'll just think of another punishment for you!'

He began to cackle his villainous laugh again.

'Ha, ha, ha! What a wonderfully cruel and heartless plan I've thought of! Oh, I'm going to enjoy your punishment immensely. Ha, ha, ha!'

He suddenly paused in mid cackle and sniffed the air around him.

Sniff, sniff, sniff.

'Hey, can anybody smell burning?' he asked. He looked at Danny, Torp and the guards who were all just standing and staring, their mouths open, their eyes fixed upon what was happening behind him.

'Stop staring off into the distance and look at me!' the professor shouted, annoyed that he wasn't the centre of attention.

'Now, where was I?' he continued. 'Oh, yes - I was cackling, wasn't I?' He cleared his throat before continuing. 'Ha, ha, ha, ha!...'

But again he suddenly paused and sniffed the air.

Escape Bid

Sniff, sniff, sniff.

'What *is* that smell? It certainly smells like burning to me!'

'That's because it is!' said a deep, smoky voice behind him.

'What?!' cried the professor in surprise. He whirled around and looked behind him.

The sight that befell his eyes turned his legs to jelly. It strangled his heart with a fearful grip and curdled the blood in his veins. Icy shivers of fear rode up and down his spine like lightening bolts.

There before him *stood* Draco!

The two guards who had been standing with buckets, ready to collect his tears, had been hypnotized by the dragon's magic. They were just standing there like statues, their eyes tightly shut.

The dragon was now completely free of the thick ropes which had held him prisoner for so many months. They lay all around his feet like twisted spaghetti, the parts he had burnt through gently smoldering. Swirling wisps of smoke drifted up from them and into the air where they danced gently upon the summer wind.

Draco had extended his wings so they were fully open, gently stretching them outwards in order to get the blood flowing through them once again. His mighty tail swished back and forth along the stone floor of the castle roof.

Free of his bonds he looked an awe-inspiring sight. He was as tall as a house, and with his wings spread out on either side, as wide as an airplane!

The professor stood there, frozen to the spot with fear.

Draco walked slowly forward towards him, his green eyes stern and angry.

'B-b-but how did you escape from the ropes?' stammered the professor in confusion.

'You're not as clever as you think you are,' said Danny. 'We wasn't trying to untie Draco as you thought. I was putting back the tooth you shot out. And once it was safely back in his mouth it returned his magic powers and he was able to breathe fire again and burn through the ropes.'

The professor gulped as the huge dragon approached even closer to him, casting him in a gloomy, dark shadow.

He quickly raised his pistol in the air and pointed it at Draco. In an instant, the dragon's eyes brightened to a dazzling, glittering green and two rays of shimmering light shot straight out - one from each eye.

The rays hit the pistol with a fizzing crack and instantly melted it, turning the metal to a hot, gooey jelly.

'Ow! Ow! Ow!' cried the professor as the scolding metal burnt his fingers. He dropped the gun to the floor and staggered backwards.

Draco advanced forward again, his eyes fixed upon the evil scientist.

'Now, now Mr. Dragon - don't do anything hasty!' whimpered the professor, trying to smile a friendly smile. However, since he hadn't had a lot of practice at smiling friendly smiles, he gave up after a few seconds as he couldn't really get the hang of it.

'Please d-d-don't hurt me!' he stammered, 'I wasn't really going to jab you with this red hot poker. I was just joking, really I was!' He dropped it to the floor and tried to adopt an innocent look.

'And what about all the other times you *did* hurt me with that poker?' replied Draco. 'Every day for the last few months!'

'Oh, yes, ah... Well...I'm ever so sorry about that. I never realized it hurt - honest! But it was just a very *little* poke, you know - just to collect a few small, tiny tears. I didn't think you'd mind.'

He laughed a nervous laugh and slowly began backing away from the approaching Draco.

'If only you'd mentioned that it hurt,' he continued, 'I would have stopped straight away. Really, I would!'

'You are a liar!' roared Draco angrily.

Suddenly Professor Zoran made a dash across the roof top and ran towards his guards who were still rooted to the spot, gazing in trepidation at the dragon. He scampered behind them as quickly as he could and then crouched down and hid, using their bodies as a barrier.

'Shoot it, shoot it!' he yelled. 'Kill that wretched dragon! Kill! Kill!'

But before the guards could raise their guns Draco opened his enormous mouth and breathed out a warning flame of burning fire into the air above their heads.

Well, this was the last straw for the guards. They weren't paid nearly enough money to take on fire-breathing dragons! There was a sudden clattering sound as they all dropped their rifles to the ground and then they all turned on their heels and ran as quickly as they could towards the wooden door at the far end of the roof.

'Stop, stop! Where are you going!?' shrieked Professor Zoran. 'You can't abandon me! Come back here at once!'

But the guards ignored him. Within a few seconds they had all disappeared from sight and were hot-footing it down the stairs as fast as their legs could carry them.

Professor Zoran stood there, nervous and afraid. He looked around him, desperately trying to figure out what to do.

'The game's up, Professor Zoran!' shouted Danny. 'You're finished!'

'Not yet, I'm not!' the villain replied as he quickly picked up one of the fallen rifles. He cocked it and aimed it at Danny!

'Now, you wretched dragon, listen to me!' the professor shouted. 'If you don't surrender to me right now then I'm going to shoot your new little friend here! I hate little boys anyway, so it will give me the greatest of pleasure.'

Draco stood still and closed his mouth, anxious not to give Professor Zoran any reason to pull the trigger.

'Well - do you surrender?'

Escape Bid

'Don't!' shouted Danny, bravely. 'He'll only kill you when he's gotten the tears he needs.'

'Shut up, you annoying little boy!' cried the professor. 'Now, dragon - do you surrender? Yes or no?'

His finger then tightened on the trigger...

Torp The Hero!

'**I** surrender,' said Draco, softly.

'A wise decision,' replied Professor Zoran with a sneer.

'I'm sorry, Danny,' Draco said, 'but I cannot let the professor shoot you. You have done enough for me already.'

Tears welled up in Danny's eyes and his lips began to tremble.

'But, but, what's going to happen to you?'

'Stop talking!' interrupted the professor. Still carefully aiming the rifle at Danny, he untied the rope around his and Torp's waists and then stepped back and turned to the little dinosaur.

'You! Go over there and pull that tooth out of that dragon's mouth! I need to take away his magic before he tries anything funny again.'

Torp glared at the evil scientist, but didn't move.

'And once that pesky tooth has been removed,' Professor Zoran continued, 'the two of you will have the

199

pleasure of holding the buckets while I collect the last few drops of tears.'

The professor sniggered and twisted one end of his long moustache tightly between his fingers. 'Oh, I'm *really* going to enjoy giving you a jolly good roasting with my hot poker.' He laughed.

'I'm going to do it long and hard. I'm going to dig it right in to your horrible, scaly skin. And then I'm going to twist it and jab it and shove it and stab it and then I'm going to ram it so hard that it will burn right through to your very bones and then I'm going to…'

He stopped suddenly as he noticed that Torp hadn't moved an inch.

'Hey - I thought I told you to go over there and get me that tooth! You better do as you're told or your friend here will get pumped full of lead.' He waved the barrel of the gun at Danny menacingly.

Torp started to walk slowly forward towards the professor as he made his way towards Draco. And then an idea came into his mind…

'That's better,' said Professor Zoran. 'You need to understand who is the boss around here. And that's me!'

He glared at Torp as the little dinosaur walked closely past him. But then his glare turned to wide-eyed surprise as the little dinosaur suddenly dived towards him! Torp shot out his left hand and hit the barrel of the gun as hard as he possibly could, sending it shooting upwards.

CLUNK!

Torp The Hero!

'Arrrgh!' squealed the professor in horror. The force of the impact was so great that the gun was knocked clean out of his grasp, sending it soaring through the air for several feet before it came crashing down onto the hard stone floor of the castle roof.

'My gun, my gun!' shrieked the professor in panic. 'You stupid little dinosaur!' He immediately dashed over to where the gun lay and bent down to pick it up.

'Hurry, Draco - do something!' yelled Danny.

But the mighty dragon had already acted. He'd aimed his mouth towards the bending professor and had opened it nice and wide. And then, from deep within his throat came a flaring plume of golden fire which burst out like a flaming rocket and shot across the castle roof and straight towards the bending Professor Zoran.

The professor suddenly felt a scorching heat on his butt.

'*ARRRGH!*' he squealed in alarm. He stood bolt up-right, the gun still on the floor, and clasped his hands to his rear.

'*ARRRGH!*' he squealed again as the flames from his burning butt stung his fingers savagely. He quickly took his hands away again and blew on them to try and cool them down.

'My butt's on fire, my butt's on fire!' he cried as he danced across the roof of the castle in panic. He skipped, he hopped, he jigged, he jived, he jumped, he pranced, he skipped and he span.

The thick flames flickered and blazed as his trousers continued to burn ferociously, lighting up his butt like a tiny yellow sun.

He bent down and tried waggling it in the air to try and fan out the fire. When this didn't work he tried turning his head around and blowing on it as hard as he could. Then he tried flapping his hands at it.

But it was no use. Nothing worked. The roaring flames continued to burn fiercely and his fiery butt got hotter and hotter and hotter.

'ARRRGH!' he squawked. *'My poor butt!'*

There was only one thing for it…

He rushed towards the edge of the roof top and then gazed down at the moat far, far below.

Lovely cooling water!

But it was a long, long way down. The professor hesitated in fear.

The surface shimmered and glistened at him in the distance, beckoning him to soothe his pain and extinguish the searing flames.

Finally the pain became too much. He took a deep breath, pinched his nose and then flung himself over the wall and right off the edge of the roof.

He began to fall…

Tumbling, rolling, somersaulting… down and down and down…

Danny and Torp hurried to the edge of the roof top and peered over the edge. They were soon joined by Draco. They all stood there and watched as the professor plummeted downwards.

Torp The Hero!

Down and down he went, spinning in the air like a Catherine Wheel.

'ARRRRRRRRRRGH!' the professor howled as he fell.

Faster and faster he dropped, until he finally reached the water and hit the surface with an almighty, sizzling splash.

SPLOSH!

Water sprayed and exploded high into the air in huge spurts and gushes. Then the professor disappeared from view altogether as the water engulfed him completely and he plunged deep down into its icy depths.

The evil professor was gone!

Soon there was nothing more to see other than a swirling circle of foamy water on the surface of the moat.

'Torp, you did it!' cried Danny as he turned towards the little dinosaur. 'You saved us from Professor Zoran!'

He walked over and gave Torp a great big hug.

'Your quick thinking certainly saved the day!' agreed Draco. 'I don't know what would have happened if you hadn't knocked that gun out of his hand.'

Torp grinned a beaming smile at them.

'I did, didn't I?!'

'Yes, you did.' Danny smiled.

'Am I really a hero?'

'Yes, you most definitely are!' said Draco.

'Wow!' gasped Torp as the realization hit him. 'I'm finally a hero! I'm a real, live hero!'

He began dancing a little jig in celebration.

Danny And The Dinosaurs

Danny and Draco laughed as the little dinosaur danced about on the roof top, wriggling his legs in the air and waving his arms about madly.

'I'm a hero, I'm a hero and now the professor's a great big zero!' he sang.

Danny and Draco both laughed loudly.

When the laughter had stopped, Draco adopted a more serious expression.

'Well, I don't know about you two,' he said, 'but I think that it's time that we left this horrible castle.' I think my wings have sufficiently recovered now.'

He stretched them out and flapped them gently up and down. 'Yes - they feel fine. Now, you both hop onto my back and I'll fly us out of here.'

Torp scampered forwards eagerly. 'Yippee, we're going home! Wait until the others hear what I did!'

He clambered onto Draco's massive back and made himself nice and comfortable.

But as Danny approached a sudden thought struck him.

What about poor Israd? She still had to travel all the way home by herself. It was an awfully long journey. Would she get back safely? What if she got attacked by a T rex? What if the river monster was waiting for her?

He quickly explained everything to Draco. The dragon listened carefully and then gave Danny a knowing smile.

'Oh, I shouldn't worry about Israd,' he said. 'I have a funny feeling that she'll be waiting for us when we get back.'

Torp The Hero!

Danny watched as Draco's eyes suddenly glowed a radiant, glittering green. The light sparkled and shimmered brightly for a few seconds and then gradually subsided.

Danny grinned a beaming smile.

Draco was using his magic to transport Israd back home!

The mighty beast winked at him.

'Now, hop onto my back, young Danny and hold on tight!'

Danny ran around and began to climb up the side of the dragon. He gripped the thick scales and hauled himself up using his hands and feet. Once safely on the dragon's back he sat behind Torp and made himself comfortable.

'Are we ready?' asked Draco, craning his long neck around to peer at them with emerald green eyes.

'Let's go!' yelled Torp excitedly

Danny leaned forward and took a firm hold of the plates on Draco's back.

Draco extended his great wings out from his body and began flapping them. And then, with a tremendous whoosh of air they lifted up into the sky and began climbing up towards the clouds at a tremendous speed.

Danny held on for all he was worth, the wind whistling around his ears like a hurricane.

The castle quickly dropped away in the distance to become nothing but a tiny speck upon the ground.

This was it, they were on their way!

A Triumphant Return!

Draco flew over the Great Forest faster than Danny thought it would be possible for any creature to fly. The dragon's huge wings beat through the air powerfully and his long tail swished behind them majestically in broad, sweeping strokes.

Danny gazed down at the rolling scenery below as it whizzed quickly by. It reminded him of his first trip in the air, when Rodak had rescued him from the T. rex in the Dark Forest. But this time his ride was far more comfortable - and enjoyable!

Soon the Great River was visible beneath them, a silvery snake of blue that wound this way and that as it crossed over the green landscape.

Danny peered down to see if the river monster was lurking about anywhere on the surface, ready to pounce upon its next victim. But all was still and quiet.

Danny And The Dinosaurs

In the distance, a flock of four-winged dinosaurs appeared into view, flying towards them in a large group.

Microraptors! thought Danny as they got nearer.

The flock saw them approaching and quickly scattered out of the way, squawking high pitched screeches of alarm as they did so.

On and on they flew…

Over the green carpeted hills and deep valleys. Over thick underbrush and rocky, volcanic terrain and through misty white clouds that covered Danny's face in tiny little raindrops that dribbled down his face.

At last, however, the familiar grass plain on Dino Island appeared into view on the far horizon.

As Danny sat there, holding tightly onto the back of the great dragon, he couldn't help feeling a great sense of pride and satisfaction that their rescue mission had been such a great success.

They'd survived an arduous and long journey, full of danger and death-defying feats:

They'd escaped from a gigantic water monster from the depths of a vast river, survived an encounter with a savage T. rex which wanted to gobble them up for its dinner, escaped from the clutches of a swampy bog, managed to evade a small army of guards in order to sneak into a castle and then, finally, they'd out-witted an evil professor and saved Draco the dragon.

The dinosaurs were safe! Professor Zoran had been defeated. His evil plan to imprison them in cages had failed!

Danny wondered what had become of the evil scientist.

A Triumphant Return!

Was he still plunging ever deeper into the icy waters of the moat? Hmm...Maybe. After all, he had fallen an awfully long way from the top of the castle. Or had he survived? Had his guards fished him out of the water and brought him back into the castle?

Danny didn't know. And right now he didn't really care about the horrible old man and his wicked deeds.

The dinosaurs future was secure. That's all that mattered right now. And he was returning in triumph!

He allowed himself a beaming smile of satisfaction as they arrived over the great grassy plain. Danny could see the dinosaurs below, as small as ants from his great height above them.

'Hang on - I'm coming in to land!' cried Draco as he made a sweeping left turn, angling his right wing higher into the air like an airplane. His great tail thrust out to one side, helping to guide him into a landing position.

Draco circled, and then they gently floated down towards the earth like a glider.

Lower and lower and lower they went...

Soon the grass was only meters below their feet, whizzing past in a blur of frenzied motion. Draco then angled his wings forward, using them as a wind break. They slowed and Draco thrust his legs out beneath him, landing with a soft thump upon the lush ground.

The thick grass swayed in the wind and massive insects buzzed and flitted about in the summer air.

Draco folded up his wings and then Danny and Torp carefully climbed down off his back.

Danny And The Dinosaurs

Dinosaurs of all kinds started to wandered close. Danny could hear excited murmurings as they gathered around. The taller dinosaurs such as the Brachiosaurus and the Diplodocus lowered their huge heads down to the ground and peered at Danny. Danny shifted awkwardly from foot to foot.

At last, Brintus emerged from the crowd.

'You've done it,' he cried and swished his tail in happiness. 'You've rescued Draco and saved all of Dino Island!'

Danny blushed from his toes to the very top of his head.

'This young human is a very brave boy indeed,' said Draco. 'If it wasn't for him, then Professor Zoran would have succeeded in his evil plan and you would have spent the rest of your lives in those horrible cages. Goodness knows what would have happened to me, but I owe my freedom to this young boy's bravery and courage.'

'Hey - what about me?!' yelled Torp, jumping up and down. 'Don't forget about me! You can't leave me out!'

Draco laughed. 'And of course, I owe a lot to little Torp, too. We all do!'

'You'll never guess what I did, Uncle Rex!' Torp continued excitedly.

'No, but I'm pretty sure you're going to tell us!' The old dinosaur smiled.

'Well, Professor Zoran was standing there and Draco had to surrender to him and then I pounced on him and he didn't know what day it was and a ferocious T.

A Triumphant Return!

rex chased us and the gun went flying out of his hand and there was this vicious river monster and his butt caught fire and I saved the day and became a hero!'

There was a pause, and then everyone erupted into gales of laughter.

Torp looked at them in surprise. 'What did I say!?'

'I think you've got your story a little mixed up,' giggled Draco.

'Did I? Well, it was like this: we were on the roof and...'

'I think you better save your account until later,' said Brintus. 'Now is the time for a celebration!'

'Did someone say "celebration?"' said a voice from the back. The dinosaurs all turned around and then a Stegosaurus slowly ambled through the crowd, a dingle-goozle leaf pressed firmly between her teeth.

'Israd!' cried Danny.

'Hello, dear!' The dinosaur smiled. 'I'm so happy to see you back safely!'

Danny ran over to her, wrapped his arms tightly around her neck and nuzzled his head into her side.

'Oh, it's so good to see you!' he said.

'Thank you, dear!'

'Did you get back here okay?'

'Well, it's funny you should say that. A most peculiar thing happened as I was making my way back through the Great Forest. There I was, trudging along and minding my own business, when all of a sudden I feel all funny and peculiar.'

'In what way?' asked Danny.

'Well, firstly I started to feel a bit dizzy and then I felt butterflies in my stomach. Oh, they were the most energetic and lively butterflies that I've ever felt! For a minute I thought they were going to burst right out of my tummy and fly straight out of my nose!'

'And then what happened?'

'My feet started to disappear!'

'Really?'

'Oh, yes, dear! They started tingling. And when I looked down at them, there they were - gone! And then my legs started to disappear, and then my whole body started disappearing before my very eyes!'

'And then what?'

'Well, I heard a sort of fizz-popping sound and then there was this big, green flashing light that sparkled and shimmered like an exploding star. And then I suddenly found myself over there by that big tree. It really was the most queer experience. I had to gobble on a few dingle-goozle leaves to calm myself down.'

'That was Draco,' explained Danny. 'I told him that you had to travel back all that way on your own and I was worried about you. So Draco transported you back here with his magic.'

'Really? Well, that explains it, then!' She turned to Draco. 'Thank you ever so much, dear. I really wasn't looking forward to traveling all that way back on my own, you know. Especially with my aching feet!'

'It was my pleasure, madam,' replied Draco, bowing his head slightly.

A Triumphant Return!

'What are we waiting for?' said Brintus. 'Let's get this celebration underway!'

He beat his tail three times on the ground. After a moment, the sound of three different beats echoed back. Then another three… then another three. Each different from the beats that had gone before. More and more dinosaurs joined in, each drumming their tails on the ground excitedly.

Faster and faster the drumming went. Then Danny started to recognize a rhythm. As the drumming reached its climax, a clear, strong voice echoed out across the plains.

'*A strange man came to this great land of ours,*' sang Brintus.
Full of trees and hills and big, beautiful flowers.
Professor Zoran was the peculiar man's name,
A villainous genius - he had no shame!

His plan was to imprison us all in cages,
The brute wanted to keep us there for ages!
And there we would stay, locked shut behind bars,
Our freedom all gone! It would no longer be ours!

But then came young Danny to help us all out,
A brave young boy, of that there's no doubt!
He agreed to undertake a most perilous mission,
He was determined to succeed in this most noble ambition.

And oh, how we cheer with the news Danny won!

Danny And The Dinosaurs

The professor was defeated - now the brute's finished, he's done!
We sing and we dance and we prance and we strut,
As the professor lies in the moat with a hot, fiery butt!'

Then Brintus began to sing the song again, with more and more dinosaurs joining in to sing the words. Danny watched as a Barosaurus approached a Triceratops and invited her to dance. Slowly, all the other dinosaurs began to dance too, and soon everyone was singing and dancing and whirling around for all they were worth.

'C'mon, Danny, let's dance, too!' cried Torp as he waltzed up to him and began twirling around. He grabbed Danny's hands and pulled him forward, skipping this way and that.

And for the rest of the afternoon, until the sun finally disappeared behind the great mountains in the far distance, they danced and they sang in joyous and blissful celebration.

Danny Says Goodbye

Danny awoke next morning to find Brintus and Draco standing by his side. He had fallen asleep under a large Calamite tree and the enormous branches were swaying gently from side to side in the warm summer sunshine.

It was a beautiful morning.

'Good morning, young Danny.' Brintus smiled. 'I trust you had a good night's sleep?'

'Good morning, Brintus,' replied Danny as he sat up and yawned. 'Yes, I had a wonderful sleep, thank you. One of the best I've ever had. There's nothing like sleeping out in the open, underneath the stars and the silvery moon.'

He smiled at Draco. 'Good morning, Draco.'

'Good morning, Danny. It's nice to hear that you slept so well.'

Danny And The Dinosaurs

'Thank you.' Danny paused and looked down to the ground. A slight frown crept its way across his face.

There was clearly something on his mind.

'What's troubling you, my friend?' asked Draco softly.

'Well, I had been wondering - before I fell asleep last night - how I was going to get back home again. With all the excitement upon arriving here and then the mission to Professor Zoran's castle, I'd not had chance to think about how I was going to get back. But now everything's over I'm feeling kind of...'

'Homesick?' Brintus asked.

'Yes. Oh, but don't get me wrong, I love it here. It's such a beautiful world and I have made some wonderful friends while I've been here. But I'm missing my parents and there isn't really much food for me to eat here. I can't live on dinglegoozle leaves for the rest of my life, although they *are* very tasty.'

'We understand, young Danny' said Brintus. 'Dino Island isn't really suited for a small boy to stay in for too long.'

'The only way back home would be the way I got here - through the hole in the magic dragon's egg. But the hole closed up right after I got here.'

He gazed sadly at the ground, picked a blade of grass and began twirling it slowly between his fingers. 'I don't suppose there's any way for me to get back now...' his voice trailed off into a despondent silence.

'Don't worry,' said Draco, 'I can get you home!'

'But how?' asked Danny.

Danny Says Goodbye

Draco grinned and pointed to his magic tooth. 'You have one wish left, remember?'

Danny sighed and scuffed the ground with his toe. 'But that only works if I'm in danger.'

'Not when I have full control of the magic,' said Draco. 'Now my tooth is back in my mouth, my magic is at full power and I can use it in *any* way that I want.'

'Does that mean I can wish for the hole in the egg to reappear?'

Draco nodded. 'Indeed it does!'

'But will the hole take me back home if I climb into it?'

'Of course. It can only return you to wherever you came from.'

'Yippee!' cried Danny, suddenly jumping to his feet in excitement. 'I can go home!'

Then suddenly, he stopped and froze like a statue as a thought struck him.

'Hang on, I don't know *where* the egg is! It was in the Dark Forest - somewhere. But I've no idea exactly where in the forest it is. Oh, no! It would be like trying to find a needle in a haystack!'

Draco smiled broadly, his gleaming ivory teeth glinting in the sun. 'Do not worry, my friend,' he said. 'I can use my magic to find it. I will fly you there!'

'Oh, thank you, Draco!' said Danny.

'It's the least I can do for all the help you've given to us.'

Danny And The Dinosaurs

'Now, before you go you'll need to eat some breakfast, ' said Brintus. 'We can't have you leaving us on an empty stomach, now can we? He grinned, before saying, 'How about some nice dinglegoozle leaves?'

Danny grinned back. 'I think I can manage a *few* more of those!'

Word soon spread around Dino Island that Danny was leaving. When the time to go arrived, a large crowd of dinosaurs had gathered together on the great plain to wish him farewell, many of them chattering and babbling excitedly amongst themselves as they patiently waited. Other dinosaurs munched on the succulent grass beneath their feet, while others dozed in the warmth of the summer sun which bathed them in its soft, yellow heat.

Brintus walked over to the crowd and gestured for them to be quiet.

'My fiends… My friends,' he began, holding his hand up in the air. He paused while he waited for the crowd to grow silent.

When they had done so, he continued.

'My friends - we are about to say farewell to a very brave boy. A boy who arrived amongst us just a few short days ago. And yet, in that short space of time, he has helped to secure our futures by defeating the evil Professor Zoran.

'No longer do we have to fear being captured and imprisoned in horrible, iron cages. Thanks to Danny,

Danny Says Goodbye

we will remain free for the rest of our lives! And for that, we all owe him a great debt of gratitude. We have also learned that not all humans are wicked and dishonest like Professor Zoran. So, please join me in thanking him. Three cheers for Danny! Hip, hip…'

'HURAY!' cheered the crowd, wildly.

'Hip, hip…'

'HURAH!'

'Hip, hip…'

'HURAH!'

Danny blushed from the top of his head to the very end of his toes. He wasn't quite sure what to say.

Then, Israd plodded out from the crowd and walked towards him, a huge beaming smile on her face. 'Goodbye, dear. I'm going to miss you terribly! It's been very nice knowing you.'

'Goodbye Israd. I'm going to miss you, too!' Danny flung his arms around the big dinosaur's neck and hugged her.

'Don't forget to pack some scrumptious dinglegoozle leaves for your journey home!' said the dinosaur. 'I've found a yummy bush just over there by that rock. The leaves are really juicy and tender. But you better hurry and pick them soon because one of those greedy iguanodons has been lurking around nearby and I have a sneaking suspicion that he's after gobbling them all up for himself!'

Danny giggled. 'I don't think I could eat any more dinglegoozle leaves, no matter how tasty they are. I've just had a load of them for my breakfast.'

'Oh, well suit yourself, dear. That means more for me, then. Well, that's if that pesky iguanodon doesn't get them first!'

Danny giggled.

'Goodbye young human,' another voice suddenly said. Danny looked over as Rodak waddled towards him from the crowd. The pterodactyl stopped in front of him and then eyed him like a schoolmaster looking at a naughty child.

'Goodbye Rodak,' replied Danny. 'Thanks for your help in finding Draco.'

'And well you may thank me,' said the dinosaur, grumpily. 'Without my vitally important information I have no doubt that you would never have found the dragon and your mission would have been a total and utter failure.'

He fluffed up his feathers, importantly. Then, he bent down and put the end of his gigantic beak close to Danny's ear and whispered:

'But you did a great job, too! Thank you!'

He then stood up again and gave Danny a sly wink.

Danny grinned back. *Rodak wasn't such a grumpy-guts after all!*

'Goodbye Danny!' cried Torp as he scampered forward. 'I'm sorry you're going. Who else am I going to go on adventures with now?'

'Bye, Torp. Oh, I'm sure you'll find someone.'

'But they won't be the same as you!'

Danny blushed again. 'Thanks.'

Danny Says Goodbye

'I'll never forget you. You helped to make me a hero for the very first time in my life!'

'I'm sure it won't be the last time.'

They hugged and Danny felt large, salty tears forming in the corners of his eyes. He sure was fond of the little dinosaur. They'd been through so much together.

Brintus then approached Danny, his gigantic feet thumping down on the soft grass as he walked.

'Farewell, young Danny,' he said. 'We'll always owe you a great debt of gratitude for your bravery and help. May your journey home be a safe one.'

'Goodbye Brintus. I'm so glad that I was able to help you all. No one deserves to be trapped in a cage for the rest of their lives.'

Brintus smiled back. 'Thank you for everything.'

'Time to go, Danny!' said a voice from behind. It was Draco, who was waiting by the Calamite tree Danny had slept under the night before.

Danny turned to look at him. 'I'm coming,' he said.

He slowly walked over to the dragon who was lying flat on the grass, ready to let Danny climb onto his back. Once he had reached him, Danny turned around to face the crowd of dinosaurs for the last time.

They all smiled back at him. Warm, friendly faces. Full of love and gratitude for what he had done for them. And there, at the very front of the crowd stood Israd, Torp, Rodak and Brintus. Torp hopped up and down and gave Danny a little wave.

Danny And The Dinosaurs

Danny felt a large lump forming in his throat. He was finding it very hard to say farewell.

A little tear then trickled down his cheek and crawled its way between his lips and slid into his mouth. The salty droplet dissolved on his tongue and he quickly wiped another tear from his eye with the back of his hand.

He smiled back at everyone. 'Goodbye! I'll miss you all!'

And with that he turned round again and carefully climbed onto Draco's back.

Once Danny was safely on top, the dragon stood up to his full height. He then opened up his mighty wings and began to beat them up and down for all he was worth. The air around Danny's ears whistled and howled as they began to rise into the air, higher and higher.

Danny gazed down at the dinosaurs below and gave them a final wave. And then with a sudden whoosh of air they accelerated upwards towards the clouds. As Danny continued to look down, the crowd of dinosaurs became smaller and smaller and smaller...

Soon they were nothing more than a blurry blob against the green carpet of the grassy plain.

Draco flew with tremendous speed. He knew exactly where he was going and within a few minutes they had crossed to the other side of Dino Island and were flying over the Great River. Danny could see the Dark Forest in the distance, the tree tops silhouetted against the sky line.

Danny Says Goodbye

As they got closer, Danny recognized the cliff top where he and Torp were rescued from the T. rex on the first day he had arrived on Dino Island.

They flew right over it and headed towards the centre of the forest. Soon, a clearing appeared ahead amidst the canopy of tree tops and Draco gradually slowed his speed, angling his mighty wings against the air. He then swooped around in a semi-circle and then glided slowly down towards the ground to land.

His feet touched down upon the ground with a gentle thump.

'Here we are Danny,' he said as he closed his wings against his body. 'The egg is not far from here. It shouldn't take us long to reach it.'

With Danny still on his back, he began walking towards a tall group of trees ahead and then they passed between them and into the gloom of the forest.

They walked for several minutes, strange animal noises echoing through their ears.

Danny wondered if they would encounter any vicious T. rex on their journey, but he wasn't frightened. After all, he was with a mighty dragon. Even a gang of hungry T. rex wouldn't be a match for a fire-breathing dragon!

Danny listened for any roaring sounds. But he didn't hear any. *Perhaps the T. rex had seen the dragon walking through the forest and had run away as fast as their legs would carry them!*

He wouldn't blame them if they did.

They traveled on and soon reached a small rise on the forest floor. Just beyond, the trees thinned, revealing the deep blue sky above. Danny could see a grassy area ahead, surrounded by thick bushes. To the right stood an enormous tree - the biggest tree he had ever seen…

He recognized it immediately.

'Hey, that's the tree!' he cried. 'The egg should be right underneath it!' And as they got closer he saw the familiar sight of the giant dragon's egg, sitting exactly where he had left it on his first day in Dino World.

Danny hopped off Draco's back and scurried towards it. When he reached it he stopped and ran his hand over the rough surface, feeling the deep ridges and furrows. But there was no hole. Not even the tiniest trace of one.

Danny turned to Draco.

'The hole's still not there.'

'Of course it's not,' replied Draco. 'Only magic will cause a hole to open in a magic dragon's egg!'

Danny nodded. Then a thought struck him.

'But if only magic will cause the hole to open, how did it open in the first place? And how did the egg suddenly grow to a gigantic size?'

He scratched his head and looked at Draco. 'Magic doesn't just happen by itself, does it?'

'Sometimes it does, yes,' replied the dragon, 'if there is a *reason* for it to happen. There is a reason for everything, young Danny. From a leaf falling off a tree to the sun shining in the sky - there is a reason behind it happening. Magic is no different.'

'Really?'

'Yes. It was your destiny to arrive here in Dino World and to travel to Dino Island to help to save myself and the dinosaurs. Fate chose you to come here, young Danny. That was the reason why the dragon's egg came into your possession, and why the magic happened to bring you here.'

'But *why* was it my destiny to come here?'

Draco laughed. 'I cannot say. 'Fate and destiny are very strange and mysterious things. Maybe one day you'll find out. But until then, just be thankful that you were chosen to carry out a very special mission.'

'I will,' said Danny. 'I'll never forget what has happened!'

'Good. Now, let's get that hole back into the egg, shall we?' Draco pointed to his tooth and smiled. 'Time to make your last wish!'

'Okay, here goes,' said Danny. He closed his eyes and wished with all of his might.

'I wish the crack in the egg would appear again so that I can go home!'

There was a moment's silence and then a small crackling noise broke the air. Danny's eyes popped open again. He looked on as the egg suddenly started to quiver and shake violently from side to side.

A small crack blossomed up the side of the egg, getting bigger and bigger until it suddenly popped open into a small hole. A hole just big enough for a small boy to climb through…

Then the egg stopped shaking and came to a complete stop, silent and as motionless as a rock as it stood there in the thick grass.

'It worked!' cried Danny.

Danny And The Dinosaurs

'Of course.' Draco grinned. 'Now - up you climb!'

'Goodbye Draco!' said Danny as he reached up and clasped the side of the hole with his hands. He then used his leg to lever himself upwards and then perched himself in the mouth of the hole.

Danny Says Goodbye

He stared inside. Darkness gazed back at him.

'Goodbye, Danny. It has been a pleasure knowing you. We'll never forget you and everything you've done for us!'

Danny smiled at Draco and gave him a final wave. Then, with a nervous breath, he jumped into the hole.

Blackness enveloped him like a thick blanket. Then he felt himself falling...

Down and down and down...

Then up and up and up!

Then sideways!

He felt the familiar fizzing sensation all around his body, just like the first time he had traveled in the egg.

Up and up he plunged. Then down again. Then sideways again.

Twisting, rolling, whirling, fizzing...

Danny felt like he was getting pulled up a waterspout the wrong way around.

Up and up and up he went. Then, with a huge sucking pop, he suddenly shot out of the hole and right back out into his Uncle Felix's attic.

He landed upon the hard, wooden floorboards with a crashing thump.

'Ouch!' yelled Danny as he rolled forwards and came to an abrupt stop against a bookcase. He lay there for a few moments while he recovered, waiting for the fizzing sensation in his body to subside.

He then sat up and rubbed his head.

The dragon's egg stood in front of him, still and silent. But as Danny got to his feet it suddenly started to tremble and shake. Then it began shrinking in size, getting smaller and smaller and smaller. And as it did so the crack in the side began to disappear.

Finally, the egg returned to its normal size and became quite still and calm once more.

Danny walked over to it. He peered down at its shimmering green surface and picked it up.

'Wow,' he whispered. *He was the only person in the whole wide world who knew just what this was. Not a dinosaur egg like his uncle thought, but a dragon's egg!*

And not just a dragon's egg, but a magical dragon's egg!

Moonlight shimmered in through the window at the far end of the room. Danny glanced at the clock - and gasped.

The time and date hadn't moved since he'd left!

Amazing! He'd arrived back in his uncle's attic at exactly the same time that he'd left!

He never realized that magic could be so clever!

Danny was so relieved. *This meant that no one would be looking for him. No one would have even noticed that he'd been gone!*

He carefully placed the egg back on the table and covered it with the black cloth. He couldn't believe he'd actually visited Dino World and no time had passed at all.

With the egg safely back in place, he crept out of the attic and closed the door behind him. He locked it with the brass key and stored it safely on the shelf next to the door.

Danny Says Goodbye

The cold air nipped at his ears as he hurried down the stairs and back to his bedroom.

As he curled up underneath the covers, a wide grin spread across his face.

This was the best summer holiday he had ever had!

Of course, no one would ever believe him if he told them that he'd traveled back in time millions of years, battled ferocious T. rex and saved a dragon from an evil professor.

But it didn't bother him at all. Danny knew...

And that was all that mattered!

Printed in Great Britain
by Amazon